THE HIGHLANDER'S CHARM

ELIZA KNIGHT

More Books by Eliza Knight

Prince Charlie's Angels

The Rebel Wears Plaid
Truly Madly Plaid
You've Got Plaid

The Sutherland Legacy

The Highlander's Gift
The Highlander's Quest
The Highlander's Stolen Bride
The Highlander's Hellion
The Highlander's Secret Vow
The Highlander's Enchantment

The Stolen Bride Series

The Highlander's Temptation
The Highlander's Reward
The Highlander's Conquest
The Highlander's Lady
The Highlander's Warrior Bride
The Highlander's Triumph
The Highlander's Sin
Wild Highland Mistletoe (a Stolen Bride winter novella)
The Highlander's Charm (a Stolen Bride novella)
A Kilted Christmas Wish – a contemporary Holiday spin-off
The Highlander's Surrender
The Highlander's Dare

The Conquered Bride Series

Conquered by the Highlander
Seduced by the Laird
Taken by the Highlander (a Conquered bride novella)
Claimed by the Warrior
Stolen by the Laird
Protected by the Laird (a Conquered bride novella)
Guarded by the Warrior

The MacDougall Legacy Series

Laird of Shadows
Laird of Twilight
Laird of Darkness

Pirates of Britannia: Devils of the Deep

Savage of the Sea
The Sea Devil
A Pirate's Bounty

The Thistles and Roses Series

Promise of a Knight
Eternally Bound
Breath from the Sea

The Highland Bound Series (Erotic time-travel)

Behind the Plaid
Bared to the Laird
Dark Side of the Laird
Highlander's Touch
Highlander Undone
Highlander Unraveled

Wicked Women

Her Desperate Gamble
Seducing the Sheriff
Kiss Me, Cowboy

Historical Fiction

Coming soon!

The Little Mayfair Bookshop

Tales From the Tudor Court

My Lady Viper
Prisoner of the Queen

Ancient Historical Fiction

A Day of Fire: a novel of Pompeii
A Year of Ravens: a novel of Boudica's Rebellion

French Revolution

Ribbons of Scarlet: a novel of the French Revolution

About the Book

They should be enemies... But passion and love know no bounds.

Returning from France to his family's manor in England, Samuel de Mowbray discovers that his two younger sisters have been stolen away to the Highlands by the Sutherland brothers. Determined to save his sisters from the hands of vicious warriors, he convinces the king to send him north on a mission. While there he discovers not only that his loyalties are beginning to waver, but that a head-strong, feisty lass could destroy everything he believes.

Catriona Buchanan needs to travel north to gain the help of her distant relations in saving her brother and ridding her castle of brutal English knights. Unfortunately, it appears the only way to escape their clutches is by trusting in the very thing she mistrusts the most—an Englishman. Minute by minute, the man who should be her enemy breaks down her defenses. There is something different about him and she can't help but be captivated by Samuel, and his steamy kisses.

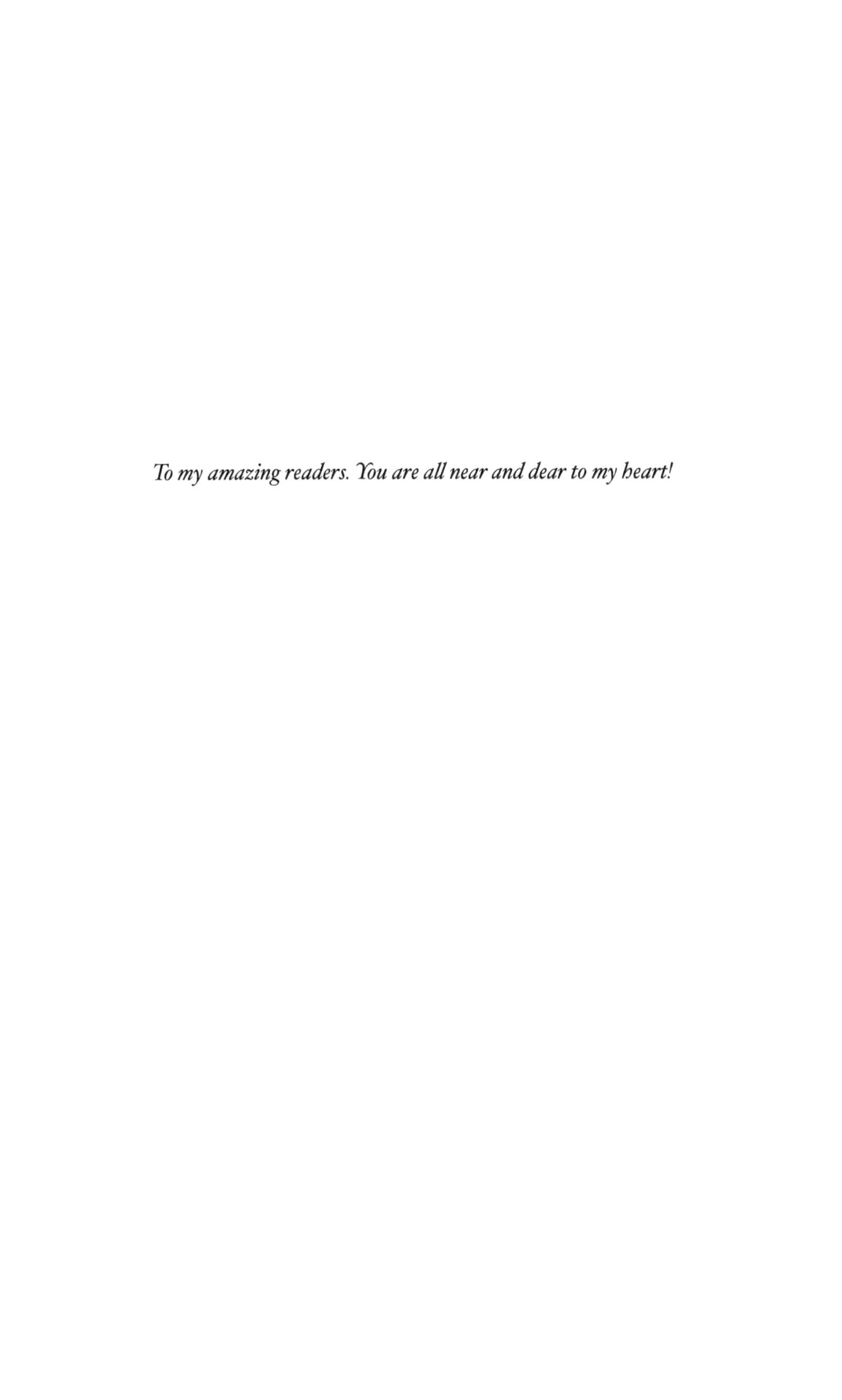

To my amazing readers. You are all near and dear to my heart!

Acknowledgments

I would like to thank all of the wonderful people who helped me in creating this fun Stolen Bride novella! My wonderful assistant, Angie Hillman. Without her I would not survive! My awesome travel and critique partner, Andrea Snider! Traveling to Scotland would not be the same without you, and neither would my books! I wish to thank my amazing and talented partners, Vonda, Vitoria, Willa and Terry, in the creation of this book! And of course, many thanks to my wonderful husband and three beautiful princesses! You guys are so good to me! Your patience is saintly!

A note to readers

Dear Readers,

I write Highland romances because I love Scotland, I love its rich history, the magic of its landscape and the endless possibilities for exhilarating tales. I'm thrilled to introduce you to Samuel de Mowbray and Catriona Buchanan. If you read, The Highlander's Reward or The Highlander's Conquest, then you'll recognize him as Arbella and Aliah's brother who was off fighting in France. Well, he's back and he wants to know what's happened to his sisters. Not only is he going to find out, he's going to fall for a little Highlander's charm himself! I loved Samuel and I really hope you do, too!

Thank you so much for reading!

Cheers,

Chapter One

CATRIONA Buchanan stood in the middle of her own worst nightmare.

Feet anchored in the center of the great hall of her family's castle, she felt her stomach drop to somewhere around her toes. At least a dozen English knights surrounded her. Completely covered in armor, their beady eyes narrowed at her from beneath their iron helmets.

At the head of the circle of Sassenachs was one man she abhorred in particular—Sir Geoffrey. These were his men, the wastrels, and they were acting upon his orders—supposedly handed down from Longshanks—to take up residence in her home. That was an outcome she could not allow to happen.

Sir Geoffrey licked his lips, his snake-like gaze roaming from her forehead down to her knees. She suppressed a shiver and swallowed the burn rising in her throat.

"Well, savage, what will it be?"

Savage? How dare he! She was no savage. The man standing before her, looking as though he were ready to rip out her heart and eat it right in front of her startled eyes, he was the savage.

Keeping her lips firm, she refused to answer his absurd question—

the bastard actually thought she might let them stay—and take her to bed for sport.

He took a threatening step forward. "We've got your walls surrounded. My men line the courtyard, and here you are all alone."

Catriona looked the man square in the eye, refusing to let him intimidate her. "Where is my brother?"

The man leered. Her brother Gregor was Chief Buchanan. Where had he gone? When the English had ridden up to their doors she'd heard him shouting orders. The fact that she was alone in the great hall with this monster was too much to take in. For it could only mean one thing—something terrible had happened to Gregor. Bile rose in her throat and she fought hard to keep her tears at bay. Do not cry now. Not with him looking. She had to remain strong. She dug her nails into her palms and bit the tip of her tongue, forcing herself not to react.

"Your brother?" Sir Geoffrey slid his fingers around the hilt of his sword, a silent show of what had occurred. "I do not believe the chief will be a problem for us, savage. I'll need your answer now. Willingly lift your skirts, else I'll have my men hold you down."

She'd never let this jackanapes or any of his men violate her. Willingly or otherwise. Catriona straightened her shoulders and lifted her chin, taking pleasure in the fact that her height nearly matched the knight's.

"Ye've no right to me. If I am the king's subject, as ye say, he would not condone your threats of violence on my person."

Sir Geoffrey let out a rusty laugh, and she had to suppress the urge to turn and flee—though where could she go? The Sassenach beasts surrounded her. Her brother's men had yet to enter, which only made her feel all the more desperate. They'd not been a strong clan to begin with. Picked off over the years by their rival neighbors. Her parents had been murdered nearly a decade before and her older brother made chief. He'd not been ready for the position, hadn't been able to build up their clan as he could have if he'd been prepared. Their father's debts had been so vast... There was barely anything left once Gregor had seen them met.

"Have you not heard the king's edict of prima nocte?" The man was moving closer.

Catriona's blood chilled at his nearness, at the coolness of his grey eyes. She'd heard of it. Heard that it was a rumor. But this man stated it as though it were fact. "I am not yet wed. Nor am I betrothed. The right is only for those women about to be married."

"Aye, and to have their virginity given to an English knight on the eve of their marriage."

She shook her head. "Then it does not apply to me."

"Oh, but it does, chit." Geoffrey turned to one of his men. "Bring him in."

Panic gripped her spine and she tried to push it aside, tried not to be afraid of what this man was implying, but 'twas impossible.

The doors to the great hall were opened and a bloodied, old man was shoved through.

"Fergus," she breathed out with fear. He was their blacksmith. A man of such great age no one was certain exactly how old he was. Widowed the previous year, he had a brood of children that could have populated one of the northern isles—at least that was what her brother had said.

"Ah, so you know this man? Count yourself lucky then that you are at least acquainted with the man whom you will spend eternity taking care of."

Catriona shifted her gaze from Fergus to Geoffrey. "What? No... I canna..."

The pain of Geoffrey's hand slapping her cheek registered before she realized that he'd struck her. "You will. And you'll do it now before God and these many witnesses."

She shook her head, desperate for a way out. "But he is not of my station," she said, hoping to appeal to what the English clung to—social castes.

"Oh, what a pity for you. 'Tis a good thing then that we English see you savages as all one and the same, as does God. I'm doing you a favor at least. I could simply rape you, then let all of my men have their turn.

But you see, I am nothing if not merciful. I will leave you a wedded woman. Is that not what all you wenches desire?"

The man was mad, sick, deranged. Not all women desired a husband, and none that she knew desired being violated or stepped on, or treated worse than the muck in a horse's stall.

"I do not desire such," she managed to say through gritted teeth.

Geoffrey shrugged. "Pity. Did your nursemaid not tell you that you do not always get what you want? My mother said it often enough." He snickered. "And now look at me"—he reached out, yanked the front of her gown so she was hauled up against him. "Now I take whatever I want."

❦

SIR SAMUEL DE MOWBRAY had not signed on to this jaunt into the Highlands to watch his superior officer violate a young maiden.

The woman embodied beauty. She was nearly tall as a man, but he guessed he had a few inches on her. Dark, sleek hair was pulled tight in a plait down her back. Her skin was pale, made paler by her fear he surmised, but her amber colored eyes shot fire. She wasn't timid—if anything she was spitting with rage. She had a good way of keeping it tightly leashed, which impressed him greatly.

It had been hard not to wince when Geoffrey slapped her. Samuel had two sisters of his own. Both of which had been stolen out from under his love-struck father's nose and now resided here in the Highlands somewhere. He was bound and determined to find out exactly where they were, too. He'd rip off their husbands' limbs and then carry his sisters back to the safety of England. When he'd arrived home after fighting the French to find that his father had gone off on something of a honeymoon with his sisters' nursemaid and that his sisters had been married off to savage Scots—brothers no less!—he about died of shock.

Getting a position within Geoffrey's unit had been a bit of a quandary, but his superior officer had finally allowed it when Samuel said he wanted to lay his blade into a Scot or two—and the king had been more than happy to send him into Scotland thinking he might be able to gain access to the Scottish rebellion leaders. Theoretically, joining Geoffrey's ranks was a step down for Samuel since he'd been at the same level as the bastard when he returned from France.

"Leave her be, ye wicked Sassenach!" shouted the old goat Geoffrey intended to wed the chit to. "God will strike ye down for what ye've done, just ye wait and see. Run, Catriona, run!"

So Catriona was her name? Had a hint of magic to it, and seemed to match her fae-like beauty.

"Somebody shut that man up," Geoffrey said with a roll of his eyes, though he did take a step back.

Relief flashed on her face, but was gone when she looked down to smooth her gown. Something in his chest tightened. The Scots were brutal bastards, worse so than his own people. Watching the woman—Catriona—be so abused by Geoffrey only pained him more in regards to his own sisters. Were they now being beaten by the barbarians who'd stolen them?

One of the knights holding the old man, bashed him on the head with the hilt of his sword knocking the man from the present.

Samuel shook his head. Blazes, but he wanted to step in. They were not here to pillage, plunder and rape. They were here to take control of the castle as the king had ordered. The small holding was nothing really on its own, but the several surrounding clan holdings when combined controlled the crossing between the Highlands and Lowlands. Having control of a major part of the border would be beneficial in gaining access and more power in the north.

How could he go about bringing up that point with Geoffrey? The man would not like to be called out in front of his own unit. Would make him look bad. Would be bad for Samuel, too, considering the leering, hungry eyes of the men watching Catriona.

"Mowbray," Geoffrey growled, startling him from his thoughts. "Take the lady to the library. Mayhap she'll be more amenable to our plans without interruption from her kin."

Samuel gave a curt nod, though he'd have to ask Catriona to show him the way. Unknowingly, Geoffrey had given him the perfect opportunity to speak with him without the prying eyes of his me. With hope, he'd be able to convince him to leave the chit alone. 'Haps appeal to his Godly side, mention what a sin it was to abuse the less fortunate and didn't he want to be seen as a merciful leader. But Samuel had his doubts a line like that would sway this brutal man. He seemed to enjoy harming others, especially those who couldn't or wouldn't fight back. Men like that were never reasonable.

Stepping forward, Samuel sighed deeply and gently gripped Catriona above the elbow. He kept his touch light, not wanting to frighten her, but by taking hold he was also showing Geoffrey what he wanted to see—the man didn't need to know just how slight his hold was.

"Show me to the library," he demanded in a low voice.

Catriona glanced up at him, her fiery gaze connecting with his and sending a jolt through him. Was it possible to be struck by lightning figuratively? Because that was how he felt. And then he was immediately disgusted. He sneered at his moment of femininity, baring his teeth at the chit. He didn't like that this woman could make him feel things he'd never felt before, and he didn't even know her.

She didn't move. But stared up at him, fear pooling in her eyes. Beneath his fingertips she wasn't warm and she trembled. Geoffrey had scared the warmth from her blood. A fierce need to protect her tugged at his gut.

"The library. Now," he bit out. For the love of Christ, he couldn't turn her over to Geoffrey. With skin so smooth, she couldn't be a day over eighteen summers, and was most likely a virgin, if she even knew the ways of men.

Her lips pressed together, crinkling at the corners as it looked like she would say something. Judging from what he'd seen it wasn't going to be pleasant, which might only cause Geoffrey to take her to the library himself.

Samuel widened his eyes and gave a barely perceptible shake of his head. Catriona appeared to understand his slight warning and instead of speaking gave a single nod, then took several tentative steps toward a slim archway off the side of the great hall.

"Where exactly is the library?" he asked, not wanting to be surprised by a room full of Highlanders. They'd swept the castle, but Samuel hadn't been on the team that had discovered the room.

"Just up the stairs," she murmured, her voice strained.

As they passed through the archway and were out of earshot of the men, Samuel whispered, "Do as I say, and I'll do my damndest to see he doesn't hurt you."

Chapter Two

THE stairwell was dark, made darker by the circular stair that tactically cut off light from above and below as a method of defense. To save coin, they only lit the torches at night and the servants within the house—however few there were—had learned to traverse the stairs in the dark.

Catriona blinked, trying to let her eyes adjust and make out the expression in the eyes of the knight who'd been charged with taking her to the library. A place she'd once sought refuge and peace in, but would now take some ungodly punishment if Sir Geoffrey had his way. She gritted her teeth. Her escort had growled a confusing promise of protection.

What could this man mean? He'd try not to see her harmed? What did he care about her?

She put one foot on the stair and then turned to look at him. Light filtered from the great hall, outlining his figure. His face was covered with metal, and it further shadowed his eyes. How could he ensure she wasn't hurt? Would he be the one to knock her over the head so she didn't feel Sir Geoffrey's rough hands on her? That was hardly what she'd call protection. Catriona narrowed her eyes. Who was the man behind the mask? For the most part, Catriona was a good judge of character if she could see their faces.

She couldn't tell if he spoke the truth or was testing her.

He stood still as a statue blocking her path back to the great hall. Chainmail covered his arms and the part of his chest where his red and gold liveried tunic dipped. The breadth of his shoulders was impressive, but she assumed it must be for him to carry all that metal—even his boots were protected by chainmail. He was taller than her. By at least a head, which was so odd to her that she nearly forgot her thoughts. Most men equaled her height with only a few exceptions—this English knight being one of them. Ugh. She hated that this goat possessed a trait she admired.

Loud, pain-filled cries followed by laughter came from the great hall. The hair on her arms raised and she instinctively took a step forward, determined to get around the metal-clad door and help whomever Geoffrey and his crew were determined to hurt. But his hand on her arms stopped her.

"Don't go out there. I can help you, but not if you put yourself in Geoffrey's sight." The smooth, deep timbre of his voice should have sent her into a rage, but instead a shiver of interest tickled the back of her spine.

She liked the sound of his voice. That might have been even more disturbing. She had to run. But how?

If she did choose to make a run for it, she'd only end up in the evil arms of Geoffrey and his men. If she went down the stairs, she'd end up in the cellar which was windowless and of little use. Up was her only option. Maybe she could find a weapon to use against him, and then make her escape.

For now, the best course would be to act as though she didn't care either way. "I dinna need your help, Sassenach," she spit out.

Why didn't he tighten his hold on her arm? Shouldn't he be itching to strike her? The English were a brutal, blood-thirsty lot. She was surprised she'd not already been raped, her throat slit.

"Get your hands off me," she demanded, yanking against his weak hold.

Instantly, his hand dropped from her arm.

What in the world...? She raked her gaze over his shadowed form. In the dim light she couldn't tell if he was bleeding, but assumed he must be injured somehow. Why else would he be so eager to let go of her? That was probably why Sir Geoffrey had assigned him as her escort, because he was too weak to finish off the rest of her people. She almost felt sorry for him. Almost. He would be very easy to overpower and then she could make her escape.

With a sigh, Catriona said, "Well, come on then. We need to get up stairs, and it might take ye a while."

The man grunted his reply and moved his arm in a dark blur toward the stairs, indicating she should go first. Probably didn't want her to see him limp. Well, served him right for the crimes he must have committed against her people.

"The stairs are oft slippery, Sassenach, and with your heavy armor and limitations, ye'll likely lose your balance. I willna be catching ye, so hold tight to the wall, else ye'll never reach the library," she warned.

"I am not limited, chit. Now up you go."

Catriona shrugged, lifting the hem of her gown as she climbed. "Limited, flawed, weak, whatever ye wish to call it."

The knight blew out a deep irritated breath. "I am none of those, and if you continue to insult me I'll be forced to show you my strength."

Now it was her turn to grunt. Obviously, she'd hit a sore spot with the poor lad. Maybe beneath all the armor he was missing a limb, or had lost enough blood that he was addle-brained. Too bad for him, it was a good thing for her.

The slim, hidden door on the left came into view and Catriona almost passed it by when a thought occurred to her. If she were to lead this man to a different place, she could easily overtake him in his state, and it would be awhile before Geoffrey and his horde of maggots found him. By then, she'd be long gone. Their castle might have been small, but it was not without its own secrets and abilities to protect those who claimed it as home.

She slipped her finger into the crack between the stone wall and the left side of the door until she found the hidden latch and clicked it open.

"This way, English," she said, cautiously keeping any excitement from her voice.

They stepped through and when the man didn't quite shut it tight enough she stepped around him and berated him with an easy lie. "Must shut it all the way. 'Tis so drafty in here, the winds have blown the door right off several times." She clicked the latch back into place, then scooted back around the metal-clad lad to lead him further down the darkened, slim hallway. Luckily the stairwell had also been just as dark, else he might have picked up on her trickery.

The stone floor was more uneven here as it was crudely and quickly made, and nary a soul had ever walked this way unless they, like she, was trying to escape. A very tiny hole in the wall at the end of the corridor lit a shaft of white light through the center of the walkway. Catriona followed the light to the end and then found the hidden latch to another door that led down a stairwell so slim she worried the knight might not be able to manage it.

"A shortcut?" he said, amusement in his voice.

She didn't like that. He was toying with her.

"Nay," she said, a little too put out. He was going to catch on to what she was doing.

"Hmm. We had a few at Mowbray Manor, but as this is my first fortress in Scotland, I'd not known you savages have secret passages."

Catriona stopped on the stairs and the knight ran right into her, the cold iron seeping into her skin and chilling her already frigid bones. She started to fall forward, but was saved by his surprisingly strong grip on her shoulders.

She cleared her throat and straightened herself, not bothering to thank him for saving her from serious injury. "We are not savages. And this is not a secret passageway."

The man was a lot smarter than she thought, and that just rubbed her entirely the wrong way.

He grunted. A sound she was quickly becoming annoyed with, and that she was also coming to associate with him not believing her nonsense. The sooner she got rid of this oversized goon, the better.

NOT A SECRET PASSAGE HIS ARSE.

Behind his helmet, Samuel glared down at the chit, though he couldn't see more than a shadowy outline of her head and body. He kept himself vigilant the rest of the descent, all too keen aware of the supple curve of her shoulders, the way her skin had heated against his palms. She'd been cold in the great hall, but was now warmer.

He frowned all the more. She was definitely up to something. What that something was, he guessed was escape, and with confidence, he'd seen it excited her. But how exactly was she planning to break away?

Then it occurred to him—she'd called him weak, limited. The poor woman had mistaken his gentleness for weakness—a realization that made him all the more scared for his own sisters. How rough were the savages with their women?

Well, he could use this knowledge to his advantage.

"Whatever you say, my lady. I but hope you lead us quickly into the library so I might find a seat." He grinned since she couldn't see it.

"Oh, aye," she said, an audible sigh permeating the stairwell. "There are plenty of seats in the library." She paused, and he resisted the urge to bump into her, just so he could feel the heat of her again seep through his cold mail. "Ah, here we are." Excitement threaded her words. She was extremely pleased with herself.

Just where had she taken him?

A door creaked open, but no light crept in. A secret room. One without windows.

"Is this the library?" he asked, stepping through after her. She'd moved quickly away from the door, familiar with the room where he was not.

"Mmhmm," she said. "Come over here, there is a seat, and then I shall light the candles."

A trick, he was certain, but he liked this game they were playing.

Feigning pain, he said, "Oh, but I fear I'll fall. I'm feeling out of sorts. Can you light the candle first?"

He heard her sharp puff of breath and could almost feel her irritation. It only made him smile more. Granted, Sir Geoffrey was an imbecile, but that did not mean that all the English had their heads up their arses and hands wrapped around their cocks. And soon she'd know just that.

"If ye insist," she said.

He could almost picture the pinched look of her as she glared at him through the dark.

"Many thanks for your hospitality, my lady," he said, praying the sarcasm did not show in his voice.

Her shadow swept from one side of the room to another and he wondered if she was unaware of where he stood, but when he felt her come up beside him, felt the whoosh of air, he put out his hands at the last second to catch her swinging arm, and grappled the fire poker from her tight fist.

"Nice try," he whispered against her ear, sliding his hands over the curve of her upper arm, and holding her only a little tighter—not tight enough to hurt. "Best be certain your prey is weak before assuming such."

The heat of their exchange crackled in the air. Her breaths puffed out hard, and she jerked, trying to free herself from his hold. Unsure of why, but unable to fight it nevertheless, Samuel had the overwhelming urge to kiss her until she melted against him. To unleash the passion he knew had to simmer beneath the surface of her fiery temper.

He held back, forcing himself not to lean forward, to lift his helmet and let his lips brush hers. Instead, he loosened his grip on one shoulder and slid his hand up to the side of her neck, touching the place where her pulse beat hard beneath the tender flesh. Feeling that little beat jump under his touch, he smiled at the inhale of her breath.

He lifted his face plate, leaned close, his nose brushing her hair, taking in the floral, spicy scent.

"What do you have to say for yourself?" he asked, his lips brushing over her ear.

She didn't move.

Didn't try to pull away.

In fact, she leaned a little closer and shivered.

If he were a daft man, and he wasn't, he might have been tricked into believing that she wanted him to kiss her. The tip of his nose skimmed over the line of her jaw. Maybe he would just take a little taste of her. A sweet kiss for the road, as he escaped this place in search of his sisters. Sir Geoffrey and King Edward be damned.

"Sir, please," she whimpered. "Please dinna hurt me."

It was those words that had him letting go, pushing himself away from her. Her shiver had not been from want of a kiss, but fear.

Disgust rolled over him in waves. What had he been thinking, touching her like that? Saints, but he'd nearly kissed her. Had drawn in her pleasant scent and been intoxicated by it.

"You're an enchantress," he murmured. And I'm a bastard.

"And ye're a bloody English boor."

That sounded right to him, but he wasn't about to let her know how he felt about his own actions. In fact, he'd best prepare her for what would happen if Sir Geoffrey could get a hold of her. "Watch the way you speak to us bloody English, chit, else you find one not so nice as myself."

She humphed loudly and walked away. The clink of iron had him guessing she'd replaced the fire poker.

"Might want to step more lightly, too. I heard every little toe tap from the moment we entered this little secret hideaway of yours." He pulled a flint from his pouch, and walked toward the outline of a hearth. With luck there would be wood in the fireplace to light the room. "What exactly did you have planned?"

"I dinna need to share my plans with ye," she said.

Samuel shrugged. On top of the hearth he found a candle and thought it might be easier to light. A flick of his wrists and the room was illuminated. It did have the look of a library, just not the one he'd been expecting.

"Right you are, my lady, but..." He set down the candlestick and turned his gaze full on her. She was mesmerizing in the golden light. "I may have a proposition for you."

The words were out of his mouth before he could think on them further.

"Proposition?"

"Aye." He nodded as the idea sunk further. "You need my help, and as it turns out, I need yours."

Chapter Three

H E needed her help?

What kind of twist of fate was that?

In the dim light Catriona took the time to really study the knight who'd turned out to be different than she first assumed. His face wasn't smooth—about a day or two worth of beard grazed his cheeks and chin. He didn't smile, but his lips weren't fierce either. In fact, they were perhaps the most handsome lips she'd ever seen. They were pink and soft looking, but shaped like a man's mouth. A mouth born for kissing.

Good lord, but what was she thinking? She wasn't obviously. She couldn't stop staring at his kissable lips and his eyes that were ice blue. Her gaze shifted back and forth. She shivered and tried to focus on something else. The bump at the bridge of his nose was a good place. Must have broken it once or twice. She frowned as she concentrated on the spot. She'd been duped by this knight. And she didn't like it.

Either he was good at faking it, or he really didn't have an injury. She was going to hazard a guess that he'd been cunning enough to figure out that she assumed he was injured and let her think so. Bastard. But what more could she expect from an Englishman? 'Twas well known that none of the English had any morals. Zounds, but she was lucky to still be alive. Once he'd figured out that she'd led him to this secret room, he could have easily ravished and killed her. And yet when he'd had his lips on her ear... When he'd nearly kissed her...

Catriona's blood heated and tingles pricked their way along her limbs and fluttered in her belly. What the bloody hell was happening? She wasn't supposed to be interested in this imbecile. Well, she wasn't. Her body was the rebellious one.

She crossed her arms over her chest and humphed. "I dinna think there is anything I can help ye with, nor do I need your protection."

The man shrugged, and she noted his expression did not change, though his eyes studied her with great interest.

"I know you think you don't need my help, but I hate to point out the fact that you're alone in a castle with nothing but Englishmen— most of whom would like to see you bent over that chair with your skirts up around your ears."

The image he placed in her mind was scandalous, and while it should have brought fear, all she could think about were his lips on her ear. She grimaced. It was his fault. All the bloody English's fault. If they'd not brought their immoral, savage selves into her castle she'd not be thinking this way at all.

"I can take care of myself."

As her lips formed the f sound in myself, he was on her, whirling her around. He wrapped one arm around her waist and pressed his other hand over her mouth. Effortlessly, he hauled her into the air.

"Let me see you take care of yourself when I've got you braced against me."

That was an invitation she wasn't about to pass up. Catriona bucked against the knight, kicked at his knees, elbowed his shoulders. But he didn't let go.

"If Geoffrey or one of his men want you bad enough, little savage, they'll have you."

To prove his point he carried her over to the table, swiped it free and put pressure on the small of her back that made her instinctively bend forward. He hadn't hurt her, but he was scaring the breath from her.

Fear sucked away any bravado she might have had before. Was he going to violate her to prove his point?

She waited for the air to hit her bare buttocks as he lifted her skirt, but it never did. In fact, it took a few moments for her to realize he wasn't even touching her. Wasn't even standing near her anymore.

"Get up, chit." His voice was gentle, almost remorseful. "I would never hurt you."

Shaking, she pressed her hands to the table and slowly lifted herself up. Throat tight, she couldn't make her voice work. Her lips trembled and teeth chattered. She rubbed at her arms and turned around to face the knight who both frightened and intrigued her. She was glad to see that his eye was already swelling where her elbow had connected. Aye, he was bigger, and dammit if he didn't overpower her, but at least she'd fought back. Just like her brother had taught her.

She clamped her teeth hard to keep them from chattering, pressed her lips even harder. There was no way she'd show this man that he'd frightened her. Catriona studied his face. His eyes didn't waver from hers. The muscles of his jaw were clenched tight, and though he stood, rigid, his hands weren't flexed. The man was waiting for her. Patiently.

It was troubling in its complexity.

"Why do ye think I can help ye?" she asked, crossing her arms protectively across her chest.

His lips quirked into a slight grin. "So you agree that I can protect you? That you can trust me?"

"That remains to be seen," she grumbled. "Answer my question."

His grin widened. "Because you're a Scot and I'm not."

Catriona narrowed her eyes. "That was obvious before, but what has that to do with anything?"

"I need to find my sisters."

She cocked her head. "I still dinna see what ye're getting at, Sassenach."

"My sisters were kidnapped by two of your brethren. I need to find them posthaste."

"By Buchanans? Posthaste?" She couldn't help but smile—though she did it closed mouthed. The man's manner of speech was so proper, it didn't suit his armor, nor the way he'd touched her.

"Not Buchanans, and indeed, posthaste, mademoiselle, if you would be so kind."

Now he was using French. She controlled the urge to roll her eyes. Swiping a hand over her mussed hair in an attempt to smooth it, she said, "I have not seen your sisters."

He shrugged. "That doesn't matter. I know who has them, and I intend for you to be my guide north."

"Guide?" She'd never been a guide for anyone. Had only traveled north one time a few years ago with her brother after their parents were murdered. They'd gone to see their distant cousins who'd helped them to regain their castle. But if she told him that, he might not take her with him, and right now he was the only chance she had to escape Sir Geoffrey's clutches. "Where in the north?"

"Sutherland."

Her eyes widened at that. "As in the Earl of Sutherland?"

The knight looked a little surprised. "Is he an earl?"

Dear Lord, did the man not know just who he spoke of? The Sutherlands were very tightly attached to Robert the Bruce, direct enemies of the English. If they had his sisters, there was no getting them back. "Aye," Catriona drew out. "He has your sister?"

The knight nodded. "Stole her away from her bridegroom and then had one of his men—his brother—abduct my other sister."

Catriona pursed her lips in thought. Her cousin Myra was married to a relation of the Sutherlands, and she'd not mentioned two English lassies being stolen by her husband's cousins. But then again, she'd not been in touch with her cousin in a long time. 'Haps it was true. But really, was it important that it be true or not? Nay. She needed to get north, too. Maybe Myra and her husband would be able to help her once more regain her castle and avenge her brother.

"I'll take ye."

"You know the way then?"

She gave a simple nod. Sutherland wasn't too much further north than Blair Castle where Myra resided with her husband. At least, she didn't think so. When they stopped at inns along the way, she'd ask just to be sure she was on the right path. Then again, staying at inns was most likely not an option with a Sassenach.

"What is your name?" Catriona asked. "If we are to be travel companions, I should at least know that much."

He grinned again. "I am Sir Samuel de Mowbray."

The name rang familiar, but she couldn't place it. Mayhap she had heard of his sisters before.

"I am Catriona Buchanan." And, if it were true that her brother was dead, then she was Laird Catriona Buchanan, but there was no need to tell him that.

Samuel stepped forward and lifted her hand, bringing it to his lips. "A pleasure to meet you, my lady."

Her breath held as his soft mouth—those kissable lips—brushed over her knuckles. A shiver stole up her arm, and as much as she liked it, she couldn't help but think how utterly ridiculous it was.

Catriona snatched her hand back. "Dinna do that again. I'm your guide not some silly lass ye can dupe with your flirtations. And that"—she thrust her finger toward the table—"will never happen again."

Samuel placed his hand over his heart. "On my honor, my lady, I shall never lay a hand upon you again." He winked and her heart seized. "That is, unless you ask me to."

She let out a startled, exasperated gasp. "Rest assured, Sassenach, such will never occur."

He grinned at her, making her both angry and curious to know what it would feel like if he did touch her—not in a threatening way, but gently, just as his lips had been on her knuckles. Her skin still tingled.

Somewhere in the distance, a bellow sounded in the castle.

"He is looking for me," Catriona said, feeling the color drain from her face. "We have tarried too long."

Samuel frowned. He looked at the ground and then back up at her. "Is it too much to hope that this is, in fact, not the library Geoffrey spoke of and that you know of another secret corridor that will lead us away from the castle?"

Catriona nodded. "Ye're correct. And I do. But we run the risk of capture."

"How?"

Her shoulders slumped. "'Tis in the storeroom."

"And where is that?"

Catriona swallowed hard. "Just off the great hall."

Samuel groaned. "Do you mean to tell me we'll have to go through the great hall—the room filled with knights—to get to the storeroom?"

Eyes wide, she stared up at Samuel. "Would it be better to hand me over to Sir Geoffrey? I promise I'll fight ye every inch." Not that she was certain that her fight would do much other than give him another swollen eye.

Samuel cursed under his breath, and turned from her, hands on his hips.

"Odds are that your general has his men searching the castle. We may get lucky and the great hall could be empty." A ripple of fear cascaded up her spine. She didn't want to get lucky. She wanted to get the hell out of here. As it was, she was going to travel all the way north in the dead of winter without a coin to her name, nor provisions, nor a cloak, let alone a horse.

"We'll not get anywhere without a mount," Samuel said, stealing her thoughts. "And you're hardly dressed for the weather."

"There is another way."

"And that is? Please don't tell me we should jump into the moat and find a boat?"

She shook her head and narrowed her brow at him. "'Tis far too cold for that."

There were more shouts from within the castle, but she was certain they'd not find them here.

"We could wait here until they are certain of our escape, and then we can sneak to the store room. Some of the crofters outside the walls have horses. We could borrow one. And here"—she opened a trunk along the side of the wall—"are some blankets we could use for warmth."

Samuel stared at her. "Do any of the servants know of this chamber?"

Catriona shook her head. "Only my brother and I."

"It's not on any castle plans that Sir Geoffrey may find in the true library?"

"Nay."

"All right. Let us get comfortable then, because they will likely not give up the search for you until tomorrow night."

"And then we shall make our escape."

"And then we shall attempt to make our escape."

Catriona moved to sit in one of the plush chairs; her grandmother had embroidered the cushions. "What will happen to ye if they find ye?"

Samuel removed his helmet and placed it on the table. She was surprised to see how light his locks were. Like golden wheat in spring. He ran a hand through his hair and shook his head. "I'll likely be hanged for it."

"Then what will ye do when ye find your sisters? If they'd hang ye now, they'll hang ye when ye return to England."

"I will have to negotiate my way back into the king's good graces."

Her chest tightened. "Ye must love them verra much."

"I do."

"I loved my brother, too." And she burst into tears.

Chapter Four

SAMUEL'S stomach was quickly unsettled by Lady Catriona's emotional breakdown.

True, he'd grown up with two sisters, but that did not mean he'd ever gotten a clear understanding of a woman's tears, or what happened inside their minds to cause such a reaction.

He reached out awkwardly with the intent to pat her on the shoulder, but then recalled his promise to never touch her again. Shifting on his feet, he cleared his throat. "You should know, my lady, Catriona, that your brother is alive. 'Haps not well, but he is still alive."

Her tears stopped almost as soon as they started and she looked up at him, glassy eyed, mouth slightly agape. "He's not dead?"

Samuel shook his head. "Nay."

"But..." She glanced toward the door as if she expected to see someone there. "Sir Geoffrey..."

"He implied, aye. A right boor he is. But they merely beat your brother and left him shackled to the stocks in the courtyard."

Catriona ran a trembling hand through her hair. "We have to save him when we escape. They'll probably leave him out there, won't they?"

"I doubt it. They'll want to hide him away where no one can help him to flee. My guess is they'll have moved him already thinking you're the one about to help him now."

"We have to go! If he's alive, we canna let them hurt him."

"Geoffrey will nay hurt your brother. The king may hate the Scots, but he sent us here on a mission and it wasn't to kill a chief."

Anger sliced over her face and she glared up at him with her swollen eyes. "What do ye mean? The king has ordered the deaths of many and turned a blind eye to the murders, rapes and other countless savage acts your men have put upon us." Catriona stood to her very tall height and marched over to him, the sad, whiney lady gone and replaced by a warrior. She jabbed him in the chest. "All of the English will go to hell for the crimes ye've committed against my people."

Samuel was grateful for the plate of armor on his chest, because her little jab packed quite a bit of power. She was so tall and lovely at that moment, he could have kissed her, but he didn't. He had to defend himself, his character.

Pressing his hand to his chest, he said, "Now, wait a minute. Don't lump me in with Geoffrey and his lot. I didn't hurt any of your people, your brother or you."

"But you are with him. You stood by while the others hurt them."

"Aye, I did stand by. And I admit my reasons for it were purely self-ish, but I'm here now, offering to help you. Simply because I was one of Geoffrey's retainers does not mean that I would stoop to his tactics, nor condone their behavior. I assure you, I've not been with him long."

"New recruit?" she sneered.

Samuel grunted. He didn't like being mocked by her. "Hardly."

She didn't ask anything further, and he didn't want to share. Not yet. He wasn't even certain he could trust the chit, let alone if they'd make it out today. And he wasn't going to risk telling her anything in case they were found.

"I willna leave without my brother." The way her shoulders were squared and her jaw jutted forward defiantly, Samuel was pretty certain he was going to have a hell of a time convincing her to do just that.

The sounds of men running through the castle echoed through the stones. Catriona looked frantically about the room and he had a sudden fear that she would run out of the room. He stepped forward, putting on a calm face and using a soothing voice like he would to a wounded animal.

"Listen, my lady," he said.

Her gaze darted to his and connected. Thank the saints.

"I know you're worried about your brother. But you need to trust me. He will not be killed, and he would be safer if you left him than if we attempted a heist with just the two of us." She was shaking her head, eyes narrowing on his.

"You just want me to take you north."

"Aye, 'tis true, I do. But I also know Sir Geoffrey and the way his mind works. Have you friends in the north? Knowing the way to Sutherland, you must."

She nodded slowly, though a shadow of uncertainty filled her eyes. Did that mean that though she knew them, they weren't people she could trust? He knew the way that felt. Geoffrey was a perfect example. One of his own countryman, a superior officer, and yet a bastard of the first order.

"Would they help you get your brother?"

She shrugged.

Samuel ran a hand over his face, glad to have the metal away from his head. "I know you don't trust me, and I don't blame you, but right now I'm the only friend you've got. I want to help you. I want us both to make it out of here alive, and I swear to you, when we find my sisters, I will help you get your brother back."

"I canna leave him."

"Catriona," his voice came out more exasperated than he wanted. "What good are you going to be to your brother strapped to Sir Geoffrey's bed?"

That got her attention. Her mouth dropped open and her face paled considerably.

"He will not let you escape the fate he had planned for you. The king ordered your brother not to be harmed. He made no mention of you." Samuel began divesting himself of his weapons, placing them within reach on the table beside his helmet. Perhaps she'd trust him more if he weren't so menacing to look at.

"He is not to be harmed?"

"Aye, as I mentioned before."

Catriona followed his weapons with her gaze and he noticed her shoulders begin to relax. He took off his chainmail piece by piece, until he stood in his breeches, boots and the thick tunic he wore under his chainmail.

"I swear upon my life, that I will not let anyone harm you, my lady." And he meant it. No woman should have to worry for her own safety against a man.

"Why should you do so much for me?"

"Because you've no one else in the world. And you are the only one who can lead me to my sisters."

There were several moments of silence and he prayed all the while that she would say aye.

At long last, she blew out a breath and glanced up at him. "All right."

Samuel nodded. "Best get some rest. We'll need it if we are to have all our wits about us when we make our escape." He gestured toward a cushioned chaise. "Sleep there. I'll rest on the floor."

Catriona walked to the chaise and sat upon it. "They willna find us."

Samuel couldn't be sure if she was reassuring him or herself, but he nodded in acknowledgement all the same. And he'd be certain to have his sword and shield near should they be found.

"We'll survive," he said. That's what he always did. He survived.

CATRIONA LAY UPON THE CHAISE, arms folded on her middle and eyes lidded. She hoped to appear asleep as she studied the knight with whom she was trapped for an undetermined amount of time.

The golden glow of the hearth set off a soft light in the room. A comforting light that played a trick with one's mind considering the angry shouts bouncing off the stone walls of the castle. She shivered with fear. Not only afraid for her own life, but for her brother. Samuel said he was shackled in the courtyard. How badly was he injured? Was he properly clothed? In the dead of winter, he could freeze to death overnight.

Samuel glanced over toward her, his gaze roving the length of her body. Did he know she was only feigning sleep? She couldn't decipher his thoughts from his expression.

He was a few inches taller than she, body trim, and from the way his Sassenach breeches clung to his thighs, and the tunic to the breadth of his shoulders, she could only imagine what the cut of his muscles looked like beneath. She squeezed her eyes shut in earnest. Why was she thinking about his muscles?

She'd seen men train before. Hell, her brother and his men walked around in their plaids with legs showing. What was so intriguing about a man who covered his thighs with fabric?

She supposed it left enough to the imagination that she itched to take it off. Itched to see what he'd look like in Scots plaid.

Nay! Nay, she did not!

Never in her life had she had these kinds of thoughts about an Englishman. First, the man had her thinking about kisses while he terrified her and now she couldn't stop thinking about him without his breeches on.

Perhaps it was simply the novelty of an Englishman who wasn't a total bastard. He had her alone in this chamber and could have assaulted her how many times? A dozen probably.

And yet, he hadn't. On top of that, she had her eyes closed. Which meant she must unconsciously trust him.

Did she?

Should she?

Her eyes popped open at the sound of shuffling.

He'd taken off his tunic… It didn't matter that he'd used it to form a pillow, what did matter was the corded muscles of his back were now facing her and she couldn't take her eyes off of the sight. Lying on his side, he gave her a good view of his naked back, and his buttocks—in his tight breeches. She pulled her eyes away from his rear toward the line of his spine, studying the roped strength, the line of his shoulder blades. He was beautiful.

Again she was perplexed. His was not the first man's back she'd ever seen, nor would it be the last. And yet, his was so much more enticing. The curve of his spine and the indent above his buttocks were mesmerizing. She found herself suddenly wide awake, and staring indecently, once more, at the way his breeches hugged the muscles of his fine arse. Quickly, she flicked her gaze away.

Oh, saints, but had she really just stared at his arse? Again?

The image of his perfect form still burned behind her eyes.

And the man was a blasted Sassenach. It could only be the work of the devil to see that a man of English descent was so enticing. In fact, she was certain of it. After all, wasn't he distracting her?

He was. And at this rate, she'd end up not getting any sleep and she'd be no good on the road. She had to have her wits about her, especially to formulate the right speech in which to entice her distant relatives, let alone the Guardian of Scotland, into helping rid her home of the English and to save her brother.

Catriona was still not entirely set on leaving her brother. If they came across him in the courtyard and no one was about, she would get him out of the stocks herself and toss him over her horse—well, with Samuel's help. Her brother was a big man—probably Samuel's size, though a bit stockier.

She hated that she'd have to trust Samuel's judgment of Sir Geoffrey. The man was the very devil incarnate and she didn't believe for a second that he wouldn't find pleasure in tormenting Gregor. God help her, but if Myra's husband couldn't help, she didn't know what she'd do. Catriona couldn't wage war against the English on her own.

Aye, she'd had to defend the castle once when her brother had gone to meet with several surrounding lairds and they'd been attacked —an attack she still firmly believed was the purpose for the entire meeting in itself, but Gregor had not believed it. He was stubborn as a mule, and had a hard time believing anyone would betray him. Catriona, however, was less inclined to believe it.

She'd been betrayed before.

"Go to sleep, chit." Samuel's voice was gruff and startled her from her thoughts.

Her eyes widened, mouth fell open. "How do ye know I'm not?"

A soft chuckle came from where he lay on the floor. "First off, you just replied. Second, 'tis the way you're breathing."

"How am I breathing?" She frowned at the ceiling, then quickly slammed her eyelids closed.

"Like you're ready to take on every enemy in the world."

How could the man read her so well when he'd only just met her? "Mayhap, I will."

"And I'll help you. But first we need to get north. And the only way we'll be doing that is if we both get some rest."

Catriona sucked in a deep breath and let it out slowly, calming herself. She loosened her muscles, cleared her mind and allowed herself for the first time in hours to relax.

Before she knew it, her toe was nudged and she was sitting straight up on the chaise a scream on her lips and a hand covering her mouth.

"Hush, wench, 'tis time to go."

All that had happened that day came flooding back to her. She was alone with an English knight in her father's secret chamber, surrounded by the enemy and her brother's life at that moment threatened. For the love of all that was holy, she'd nearly given away their hiding spot with a scream.

She nodded, and Samuel removed his hand.

"I apologize for touching you, my lady, but I couldn't allow you to scream." He'd dressed once more, weapons glinting, and was scrutinizing her in a way that made her feel... odd.

All around them, the castle made no sounds.

"Come, my lady, we must make our escape while the devil still slumbers."

"We aren't going to wait until tomorrow night?"

"Nay. The longer we linger, the more likely we'll be found. Already they come knocking on stones."

Catriona shuddered. Sir Geoffrey must have surmised there was a secret chamber. She nodded up at Samuel. He might be her enemy, but at the moment, he was also her protector.

Chapter Five

THE sound of the door latch clicking echoed so loudly in Catriona's ears that it could have been the entire south tower collapsing. She winced, stilled and waited for the sounds of English knights signaling the alarm.

She gave a sideways glance to Samuel, certain he would be glowering at her for her fault, but instead, he had his head cocked listening, his hand on the hilt of his sword. Then he nodded at her to proceed.

They wouldn't speak to each other until they were a mile away from the castle, and only then if they had no one following them. At least that was the plan they'd come up with before she'd opened the latch. Each of them had a task to complete if they were to make it out of the castle alive. Catriona wasn't about to be the one to spoil it, and she highly doubted that Samuel would either. He'd sealed his fate the moment he made a deal with her. Whether he liked it or not, Sir Geoffrey and the rest of the English bastards would see him for the traitor that he was.

Sad really. She kind of felt bad for him. All the poor sot wanted was to find his sisters who'd been stolen away. The men who'd taken them had to be daft, for who would want an English lass? Catriona had heard plenty about them. Cold, dispassionate, rude, self-centered—

Samuel nudged her shoulder and Catriona jumped at the prompt. Time to go. Time to set aside her musings and find a way out of this hell-hole that had once been her home—and would be again if she had anything to say about it.

She shuffled forward in the dark, feeling her way along the narrow corridor, her fingers catching on spider webs and moss that grew in the cracks of mortar. They made their way forward, but not to the stairwell she'd brought him in from. Nay, there was a better way out, and she was annoyed at herself for not thinking of it before. She found the latch and it clicked, letting the hidden door slide forward barely an inch before she stilled to listen.

A shiver stole over her as she thought about her brother. 'Twould be a month or more before she'd return, for the trip north would take easily a week and a half if they rushed, and two if they were caught in any storms or had to lay low from the English.

Samuel prodded her again and she slid the door open, saying a silent prayer that the room beyond them was black as night. No one used this private chapel that her father had built beside the great hall for two reasons. One, her brother preferred to use the chapel with his people. He never prayed alone, but believed that the prayers of many were heard all the more loudly. And the second reason—her father had died here.

Catriona sucked in a ragged gasp, recalling seeing the blood covering his shirt. His hands were pressed to the wounds and he'd stared at her with vacant eyes as his mouth fell open. She squeezed her eyes shut against the memory. Now was not the time to remember such things. Now was the time for moving forward.

She felt around for the small wooden benches, and slid her fingers along the length of one until she found its end. The middle of the small chapel. There were six short benches, three in a row along either side. When she was a child, they'd had family Mass here every morning except Sunday, when they joined their clan at Kirk Buchanan.

Passing three benches, the small door to the great hall should be... her fingers brushed the wooden slats. This door was covered by a nondescript tall bookshelf, making it heavy. She feared it would creak when she pushed it. Catriona leaned her ear against the door, listening for anything she might hear beyond, but there was nothing. Once they opened the door, all they'd have to do was walk about twenty paces to the left and they'd make it to the storeroom. Once inside they could bar the door and then slip behind the barrels that hid the entrance.

But it didn't look to be their lucky day. Footsteps sounded in the great hall, and low voices.

Catriona felt for Samuel's arm and squeezed—the signal that they were not safe to move.

They waited silently, breaths so slow and ragged she was afraid she might pass out from the exertion of it.

But soon the voices faded and so did the footsteps. If they didn't make a run for it now, they never would.

She turned the handle and thanked God for her brother's insistence of the chapel's upkeep. The hinges had been well-oiled despite their lack of use. The hearth held a banked fire, and there was one candelabrum with all sixteen candles lit, but other than that, the room was cast in shadows—their corner being one of those. She slid out against the wall, and nodded for Samuel to do the same. They moved at a slow pace, uncertain of who else lurked in the darkened spots of the room. No one stopped them. No one jumped out at them shouting halt.

Five more feet and they'd be at the storeroom door. But what if someone was inside? Being the dead of night, it wouldn't make sense, but she couldn't push it out of the realm of possibilities. Sir Geoffrey could have demanded a platter of cheese and a jug of wine as a midnight snack. Greedy bastard that he was.

Catriona counted her steps... Fourteen. Fifteen. Sixteen. Seventeen. Only three more to go. A door opened—perhaps from the front entry of the castle. The creek of the hinges echoed. Funny that her brother hadn't bothered to oil those hinges. They were about to be caught, she could feel it in her bones.

Before she could protest, Samuel grabbed her hand and yanked her the last few steps and through the door. He whipped her around and closed the door behind them. His body was pressed hard to hers. They were completely encased in darkness, but she didn't need light to see, not when she could feel every hard, cold, metal-clad ridge of him pressed intimately to her.

Thick thighs pressed through the layers of her gown against her own. His pelvis dug against hers—and the hardness there sent a chill sweeping over her. She bit down on her lip, her chest heaving, and with every breath, her breasts pushed harder against his chest. Could he feel the beat of her heart? For it thumped so hard against her ribs she was certain it bounced from her bones onto his. Better question—why did she like the way it felt to have him pressed to her? Why did she want to wrap her arms around him and tilt her chin up for the press of his lips?

If they weren't running for their lives, she might have been bold enough to ask for a kiss. Hell, what was she thinking, might have? She wanted one—she would have asked. She wanted to arch her hips to get a better sense of the tingling that was slowly spreading through her core. She had to dig her fingernails against her palms to keep herself from sliding them up his spine, ripping off his helmet and running them through his golden-colored hair.

Was Samuel having similar thoughts? Through the metal of his helmet, he breathed hard. His chest rose and fell in time with hers. He didn't move. All indications that maybe he, too... What? To even ponder any of it was ridiculous. They were in grave danger of being found out.

Footsteps fell outside the door and she felt the jiggle of the handle against her back. Samuel slammed his hand against the wood and she bit down hard on her tongue to keep from yelping.

"Busy in here," he said in a gruff voice, disguising his own. "Don't worry, I'll save some for you."

A short laugh sounded on the other side, but inside the storeroom Catriona heard nothing save the beat of her own wild heart. Samuel held his breath and so did she, both knowing that if the jackanapes on the other side decided to press the issue and raise the alarm, they had little recourse.

"I'll give you another quarter of an hour, you bloody bastard, afore

I come in to try the piece you're keeping hidden away." The man's voice was slurred, drunken on her family's wine.

"I'll be sure to keep her breathing for you," Samuel said, adding a cruel laugh she'd not heard before and didn't care to hear ever again.

"I'll enjoy her whether she breathes or not," the man said, then walked off.

Samuel's cold helmet pressed to her forehead as he let out the breath he held, mingling it with her own. A close call. Too close.

Catriona pushed against his shoulders, taking note of the pure strength coiled there, but working hard not to linger.

She rushed to the far side of the storeroom, feeling her way to the barrels at the end. She struggled for half a second trying to lift a barrel before Samuel was there to help her. How he'd found her in the dark was a miracle. Once the barrel was off of the oversized one below it, she pulled off the big one's lid and bent over it until she felt along the empty bottom. There it was, a little tab. She tugged on it and the false bottom drew upward.

She tapped Samuel and broke their rule of silence, whispering. "Ye have to go first so I can close the lids."

"Inside?"

"Aye, the barrel has a false bottom. There's a ladder that leads down to the tunnel."

"I don't know if I'll fit."

"'Twas made by my grandfather. He was the size of a barrel himself. Trust me, ye'll fit."

Samuel climbed inside the barrel. Not a breath later, Catriona climbed inside, too, her foot tapping against his head.

"Sorry," she whispered, breaking their rule once more.

Samuel chuckled, but continued to descend, and took hold of her bare calf with his firm grip, and placed her foot on the first rung. She felt for it with her other foot, ignoring the heated touch of his palms on her bare skin. Steadied, she replaced first the top lid, and then descended enough to replace the false bottom, making certain to tug the tab so it didn't stick up and warn anyone of its existence.

Down another half-dozen rungs, she touched the floor of the

tunnels and gripped onto Samuel's hand. "Duck down," she murmured, and then she ran, tugging him behind her.

Curses sounded from somewhere above as the drunken knight realized he wasn't going to bed any unwilling wench. No doubt he'd pass out without realizing he'd been duped, probably just thought the knight didn't want to share and had slipped off somewhere else.

Fifty paces down the tunnel and they came to the end—a metal grate. Moonlight glinted down from the shaft of the well and lighted through the gaps between the bars. Once opened, one wrong step and they'd drown.

Catriona pulled the pin from the grate and slowly let the metal down by her feet so that it didn't make a clanging sound when it landed.

"A well?" Samuel asked.

"Aye. But dinna worry, no one is likely to be getting water at this time of night."

Samuel grunted.

"Ye go up first so I can put the pin back in."

Samuel shook his head, but in the darkness she couldn't see his expression. "You go first. I'll put the pin back in."

They didn't have time to argue, and given that she knew the lay of the courtyard better than he, she agreed. She handed over the pin and then stuck her head out, staring up into the night sky and the bucket that was tied to a rope at the top. Overhead the moon was full. A bad omen? She refused to think about it that way. Mouthing a prayer, she reached overhead and grabbed onto the first metal rung that had been secured into the stones—and promptly yanked her hand back. The rung was like ice, and oddly felt like it burned her palm. So cold it was hot. She shook her hand and gritted her teeth against the pain. She started to climb, but when she was just to the top she waited for Samuel. He'd already gotten the pin in and started to climb, too.

Knowing he was on his way up, she cocked an ear and listened. The usual night sounds flitted through the air. No voices. No horses. No footsteps. Holding her breath, she peeked over the side of the well and scanned every inch of the courtyard—every building, every corner, every bush. All appeared calm in the night. On the battlements of the wall and castle were roughly a dozen guards—half on each. They would guard well the castle they'd stolen, but none appeared to be looking down at the courtyard, instead staring off into the distance. She forced herself to glance toward the stocks, but they were empty, just as Samuel had predicted they would be. Dear Lord, but she prayed that meant Gregor was indoors and at least alive. She prayed that he lived long enough to give her the chance to save him.

"Guards," Catriona whispered.

Samuel didn't respond, only nodded.

Time for a leap of faith, bracing herself for the cold, she climbed out of the well and crouched on the ground beside it.

Chapter Six

IF they weren't in imminent danger, Samuel might have taken a moment to admire the woman who leapt out of the well above him as though it were a feat she took on daily. He'd worked hard not to glance up, else in the moonlight he capture sight of the silky, curve of her legs. He still remembered vividly how her calf had felt beneath his palm when he'd guided her foot to the rung inside the barrel.

But, there was no time for admiration or lusty thoughts for that matter. He peeked over the top of the well and took in the guards upon the walls. None looked their way, but that didn't mean they wouldn't alert them with their movements.

Catching Catriona's eye, he handed her his sword, afraid it would clang against the stone when he climbed out and not willing to let that small mistake give away their escape.

He slipped out and over the side to crouch beside her. The well was large, nearly a man's height in diameter and easily four feet from the ground up. Impressive—and it only made hiding behind it easier.

Inside, they'd discussed that the best way to escape from here was through the water gate near the south entrance that lead toward Loch Lomond. From there, they could walk along the marshy shores until they found a horse, which she assured him wouldn't be too far since there were many in their clan who lived close to the water in order to fish.

Catriona elbowed Samuel and handed him back his sword. She pointed toward the wall about fifteen paces away. What they were doing was risky, but they had no other choice. He had to find his sisters and she needed to gather forces to get her castle back.

And then she was gone, slipping unseen and unheard over the muddy courtyard to the wall where shadows enfolded her. Samuel waited to see if any of the guards would take note of the sudden movement, but none did. His turn.

He sheathed his sword to hide the glint in the moonlight, but held tight to the hilt so that it did not clang and give away his position. As he ran, he, too, kept to the shadows. Once tucked against the wall, he threw out a breath and gazed up at the guards. Nothing.

Samuel shook his head. Geoffrey's guards were lazy maggots. Even though they'd stuck to the shadows, his own men were trained to pick up through their peripheral vision anything unusual—and the two of them climbing out of a well and running across the courtyard was definitely in the realm of unusual.

They stayed pinned to the wall for the count of sixty, and then slid painfully slow along the wall, beneath stairs, behind outbuildings. Finally, they reached the south water gate, only to be confronted with it being locked. But what should he have expected? Why wouldn't it be locked? He cursed under his breath, braced his hands on his hips and shook his head. They might as well announce their presence now, because there was no other way out—

Catriona pulled a large iron key from somewhere in her skirts and slid it effortlessly into the lock. She glanced back at him and he could have sworn she winked. Samuel shook away the shock—and the need to kiss her with relief. She pushed open the door only enough for the two of them to squeeze through and then silently closed it again.

A steep, slippery, set of stairs greeted them. Flanked by two short stone walls, anyone could be seen walking up and down from the battlements above.

Shocking him once more, the woman sat on the first stair and scooted down a few before turning around to stare up at him. This was madness. Pure madness. And yet, incredibly clever. He sat down and scooted his way down, like he had as a young boy still chasing after frogs.

A shout on the wall had them stilling, and Samuel watched as Catriona tucked herself against the half stone wall, nearly melting into the rocky surface. How many times had she snuck out of here before?

His blood ran thick with alarm as the shouts continued, only louder. Had they been seen? Had their secret room been found out? Some other thing disturbed?

But then there were answering calls and Samuel realized the men were changing shifts and calling out to those they were replacing.

He shook his head for what had to be the hundredth time. Geoffrey truly was a poor leader. Any enemy watching—himself now included—would know when the men changed guard and how to easily slip past them. Which, was now.

He nudged Catriona. "Hurry, my lady," he whispered.

She wasted no time in scooting more hurriedly down the steps and when she'd reached the marshy shores of Loch Lomond, she alighted on her feet and took off at a crouched run.

Samuel followed, continuously looking backward to make certain they were not spied as they made their escape. A quarter mile around the loch and they came upon a small cluster of crofts. Hints of peat smoke curled from their chimneys, but they were otherwise quiet. In the dead of winter, the animals were housed within the croft, and so they would have to knock in order to borrow one. Samuel was not pleased about this part of the plan.

The more people who saw them leave the worse off they were, and the more danger they put those people in.

Catriona hurried to the center door whose hearth smoke curled into the night sky and gave three swift knocks. Her breath puffed out silvery in the moonlight. Because of their exertion, she'd not yet started to shiver, but she would soon. Beneath his armor, Samuel was well clothed. Besides, he was used to being out in the elements. A lady would not be. All she had was a blanket from the castle, and though it was thick, it wasn't enough protection.

"Ask for a cloak," he whispered.

She shooshed him. "Go stand back there, else they take their swords to ye."

He frowned at that. Why would a crofter have a sword?

The door opened and a burly, bearded man stuck his head out, an axe gripped tight in his hand. When he saw that it was Catriona, he lowered his weapon.

She whispered to him, and looking both ways outside, the man ushered her inside. His eyes settled on Samuel, but Catriona must have told him he wasn't a threat for he didn't call out an alarm, simply glowered. A few moments later, she emerged with a thick wool cloak about her shoulders and then they disappeared into the barn. She exited with two horses and the Scotsman behind her. The large man bypassed the horses in his intent to reach Samuel.

"The lady says ye're to keep her well and escort her to help in the north with her relations."

Samuel nodded.

"'Tis good. My family kept hidden when the English came through, else we'd be in the same predicament as a lot of folk." He jerked his head toward a croft down the road. "Tanner's wife was... well. She wishes she were dead and 'tis all he can do to keep her from jumping into the loch."

Samuel swallowed hard. It was his countrymen who had done that. Men he rode with. "I'd never hurt a woman."

The man kept his narrowed eyes on Samuel, not accepting nor denying his words. "I'm letting her borrow the horses. Not ye. See that they are returned to me. I'd give everything for the lass and her family, but I'd be happy to see the likes of ye ground to muck beneath my shite."

Again Samuel nodded, knowing instinctively that anything he had to say would mean naught.

"Keep her safe, else ye'll have the lot of us to deal with."

Samuel gave a curt nod and held out his hand. The Scot stared at it for longer than necessary before turning away. But Samuel wasn't affronted. He understood the man's disrespect. He had no cause to trust Samuel given that he had arrived with the men who now put his chief and Catriona in danger, had hurt members of their clan, but he needed this man, all of them to understand that he was not a part of that.

Aye, she'd likely be distraught when she found out that beyond gathering his sisters he was to bring back the names and locations of the rebels of Scotland, but he'd never hurt Catriona. When he returned to England, he'd simply have to explain to his king that gathering that information under Geoffrey's lead was impossible. That he'd had to break away from his regiment in order to do his bidding to his sovereign. Knowing Longshanks the way he did, he'd be able to get away with that—if he gave him what he wanted. When he'd crossed the border of England into Scotland he'd been absolutely clear on his mission. But somewhere in the past twenty-four hours something had changed.

"I'll keep her safe and return her to you. That I swear." Samuel waited for the man to turn and acknowledge him, but all he got was a nod before the man checked the saddle of Catriona's horse and whispered something to her.

"Come on, Sassenach," she teased. "We must be away afore your brethren decide to search the area for us."

"They are not my brethren," he grumbled.

They weren't. Not the bastards who followed Geoffrey. But the English were, and he was loyal to his king. And yet, he was finding it harder to say exactly why. The Scots may be heathens, but from what he'd come to see so far, they weren't as bad as his king had made out. Before Gregor Buchanan had been bashed in the head by Sir Geoffrey, the man had fought the way Samuel did. With honor, precision. Samuel's respect for the man had been solid. His people cared for him, were loyal. Gregor's sister was not unlike his own two sisters. This was a strong group of people which meant they were led by a strong leader.

But what did he really know of them? Nothing.

He leaped onto the back of his borrowed horse. "Lead the way, my Scottish guide."

Catriona let out a short laugh. "Be prepared for a grueling trip, Sir Samuel, for we are close to a fortnight from our destination."

A fortnight alone with the scamp.

He'd be lucky to make it out sane.

WHY DID she have to mention just how long she was about to be with this man? A stranger? A dangerous stranger?

Catriona nudged her horse into a gallop and they headed down the marshy road that ran the length of the loch. They'd avoid the MacFarlane's on the left of the loch and stay on the MacGregor side as her clan had entered into talks of an alliance with them. From there, they'd head up into dangerous Campbell territory.

If it weren't for the fact that she'd agreed to help him find his sisters in Sutherland, she'd make a stop to see the MacGregor and beg for his help. Hmm, maybe she should do that all the same. Then again, the MacGregor was intent on getting his hands on Buchanan land as it covered quite a bit of fresh earth near the loch—good farming land. It didn't matter that her mother had been a MacGregor, or that her brother was named after their clan. Their uncle was a bastard of the first order.

They were probably not her best choice. Her best bet was with her distant relations in the north who could help her and her brother and cared more for them than their land.

She glanced behind her. The Sassenach knight had a good seat on his horse. At least he had that going for him—along with his many other admirable attributes. Ugh, why was she thinking anything worthy about him at all?

If they actually made it all the way up to Sutherland—bypassing any other English, outlaws or raiding clansmen on the road—it would be a miracle. As slim as their chances were, she had to try. Had to save her brother and her clan.

They were depending on her, and at that moment, she was all they had left.

Dear lord, but she hoped Gregor would be all right. He had to be. He was all she had left.

The trees along the road reached out overtop of them, like long, hooked fingers ready to reach down and pluck them from their horses. Catriona shivered, and used one hand to tuck her borrowed cloak tighter around herself and the blanket tighter on her legs. The crisp, wintry air smelled like snow. It'd been at least a sennight since the last snowfall, and she'd be surprised if flakes didn't start falling by daybreak.

Just another mark against them.

Indeed, it would be a miracle if they made it.

Chapter Seven

CATRIONA glanced down at her hands gripping the reins like a lifeline. Her knuckles were white circles, surrounded by red, angry flesh and her nails purple from the cold. The incessant clicking of her teeth as they chattered rivaled the ping of ice against the tree limbs above them.

When the ice had started to fall just an hour after dawn, they'd moved within the trees hoping the forest would block much of the storm. She was glad they had, because for certain if they were still out beside the loch, they'd have long since turned to ice themselves.

"We should seek shelter," Samuel called out above the din.

He didn't sound as cold as she felt. She turned slowly to the left to see him riding beside her. He didn't look as cold as she felt either. Blasted English. She was supposed to be the heartier of them both, and yet he looked as though he were out for a leisure ride in spring. His armor glinted with ice frozen to the links. How in the bloody hell...?

Catriona nodded, thinking that the flames of a roaring fire sounded like heaven.

They'd not yet passed an inn, and she was beginning to wonder if they would. Already they'd entered Campbell lands, and likely if they did find an inn, the owners would not be hospitable to them for two reasons. One, Samuel was English. Two, her brother and Chief of the Clan Campbell had a bit of a tiff the month before when Campbell's son asked for Catriona's hand in marriage. Her brother had considered it briefly before simply laughing him off. But not before the man had a chance to try and seduce her... His bruised ego had been loudly exclaimed through all of Scotland.

But she was glad to not have been linked to the brute.

In fact, she was perfectly happy to remain in her brother's home forever.

Well, as long as it wasn't full of English bastards.

"I dinna... know... where... we can... stop," Catriona said. She blinked rapidly, trying to warm the icicles that had formed on her eye lashes.

"The first place we see," Samuel said. A frown marred his brow as he examined her.

He must have thought her weak. Well, she wasn't. She was strong. She simply couldn't stand the cold, and any normal human being would be in the same state as she—save for him. But he wasn't normal. Samuel wasn't a bastard like his counterparts, and yet he was apparently cold-blooded as he was thriving in this awful weather.

Catriona nodded her agreement, though at this point she was starting to doubt they'd find a place and that she'd ever witness a dawn rising again.

She closed her eyes, afraid they too might freeze, and then popped them open when her horse stumbled. Even the poor animals were beginning to be affected by the rough weather. Her borrowed mount had ice on his lashes, crisping his mane, and it had been a while since he'd been able to do anything more than walk. Even hearty Highlanders like herself knew when it was time to seek out shelter before the weather proved deadly.

What felt like hours later, but in reality may have only been a few moments, they passed a young man chopping wood beside a croft.

"Ye look to be frozen there, lass," he said to Catriona, but his voice trailed off when he caught sight of Samuel. "Well, it's no wonder with an Englishman holding ye captive."

The lad was bold for his age—pushing at least twenty summers by the look of it. Only a year or two younger than herself.

"Would... would ye mind... terribly, if we... we warmed ourselves by your fire?" Catriona asked. She gestured to Samuel. "He... he is a friend of mine. Though he is English, he is not like the rest of... them."

She gazed back at him, realizing that even though she'd said it to get into the warmth of the croft, she meant it. And that bothered her. Samuel was proving to be nothing like what she'd grown up to believe the English were like.

The thought was disturbing.

"Come, I'll check with the others."

The young man took his bundle of wood back inside the croft. A moment later, a large man—rather resembling a giant from childhood tales—stepped from within the croft. He had to be close to seven and half feet tall. He held an ax and pressed it against his opposite palm.

"As God would punish us for turning ye out into the cold when ye're nigh on frozen to death, we'll let ye stay the night, but the English has to sleep with the horses."

Catriona sent a pleading glance Samuel's way and was surprised when he readily agreed.

"Our thanks," Catriona said to the man. "I am Catriona, and this is Samuel."

"We dinna want your names, nor shall we give ye ours. If anyone comes looking for ye, we'll know not who ye were and if ye be captured ye canna tell who it is that helped ye in your escape."

Catriona opened her mouth to argue, but the man held up his hand. "Dinna bother, lassie. No sane man or woman would be out in weather like this with company like him unless they were running from someone."

He had a point, and the heat from the croft beckoned. No use in arguing.

The giant took hold of Samuel's reins while he dismounted and the younger man helped her to get down. They took their horses inside first leading them into the byre with several farm animals and a horse of their own. The giant nudged Samuel into that room, but beckoned Catriona to warm herself by the fire.

"Might my friend warm himself before bedding down with the pigs?" she asked, trying to sound pleading rather than offended. She gave a small soft smile and a shrug of her shoulders, hoping her feigned naiveté would hit a mark with their host.

The giant grunted, his gaze flicking to the door. She took that as a yes.

Though she'd rather stay and warm herself, she hobbled on numb feet toward the side room. Samuel was brushing down the horses, already having removed their saddles. His weapons and tunic bearing Longshanks crest were piled beside the saddles.

"They said ye can warm yourself first."

Samuel's lip quirked in a half-smile but he shook his head. "Go, my lady. I'll be fine here."

But she didn't want to go. Didn't want to leave him to freeze. "Just a few moments?" she asked. "For me?"

She hid her surprise when he ducked his head to hide a pleased smile. He did want to be by the fire she was certain, but male bravado often won out over basic needs. When she'd invited him to join her—because she needed him—it gave him an excuse to push that bravado away.

Catriona was not an expert in men, nor the male mind, but having grown up with her brother, who was particularly full of ego and bravado, she'd learned a thing or two.

"Well?" she prodded.

"If it would please you, then aye." Samuel unbelted the sword at his side, settling it against the wall. "Wouldn't want to offend them," he said with a nod of his head toward the giant Scot.

They walked back into the main room of the croft where the giant stoked a raging fire in a rather large hearth. Hanging over the blaze was a pot full of something succulent smelling. He was surrounded by what appeared to be his family—a woman about his age, the young lad, four other young boys and a tiny little girl no more than a few summers.

The man had yet to set down his ax, and his boy carried a cudgel. The tension in the room was thick as a whip and would strangle them if not calmed.

All eight of them stared warily at Samuel and Catriona as they made their way to the fire. She pretended their hosts weren't holding weapons, nor that she and Samuel were currently at their mercy. Hopefully they'd take note that Samuel was unarmed.

Catriona's stomach growled. Whatever was in that pot would taste delicious right about now, even if it was a boiled boot.

The woman of the house cleared her throat. "We'll sup in a few moments. We've not a lot, but enough to give ye each a bowl."

"Many thanks, to ye," Catriona said.

"Aye, much thanks for your hospitality." The sound of Samuel's voice startled the woman and she swiveled an angry glare at her husband who mouthed something unintelligible.

The heat of the fire distracted Catriona from their exchange. The warmth of it was so intense upon her frozen limbs it stung. She rubbed her hands together, feeling the ice on her bones begin to melt. Beside her, Samuel did the same. It was all she could do to keep from moaning a contented sigh.

She shifted on her feet as all the cold from outside melted away leaving tingly warmth in its path. Samuel nudged her with his hip.

"Warming up?" he asked under his breath.

"Aye. Ye?"

"Mm-hmm. Any places that you have no feeling?"

Catriona did a body check. Nope. She could feel everywhere. "Nay."

"Good, so you'll likely not lose a toe from our travels."

She raised a brow. "Have ye known someone to lose a toe before?"

With a serious nod, Samuel said, "Aye."

Catriona cocked her head, suddenly wanting to know more about this Sassenach. "Who?"

"A man in my regiment. 'Twas last winter in France." He rubbed his hands vigorously before the fire. "Lost two of his toes and his little finger."

She couldn't help the surprise that surely registered on her face. "I didna know France could be so cold. Ye were exposed to winter without shelter?"

He gave a gruff laugh. "You don't know much about warfare, do you?"

She frowned. "I know something of it. I wouldn't have met ye otherwise."

Samuel narrowed his brow. "That was no warfare, my dear. In war, there is actually a battle fought. Sir Geoffrey likes to strike his enemies in the back. I give mine fair warning."

"And nearly froze to death doing it?"

He shrugged. "I only do my duty to the king."

"And do ye ever think that mayhap your king is wrong in his desires and requests of his people?"

Samuel cocked his head in thought, holding his hands closer to the fire. "There are times."

His response was simple and curt, but it resonated deeply within her. "What will ye do?"

A small bowl of soup was thrust into her hands, and then another into Samuel's. No spoons were given, and so they sipped it slowly. The family was content to ignore them, which Catriona was happy to respect since they'd opened up their home, hearth and pot to them. The soup warmed her from the inside out. She was actually starting to feel somewhat herself again.

Samuel stared at her over the rim of his soup. "I don't know."

"Ye could always be an outlaw." She grinned.

He raised one brow and gave an exaggerated nod. "I am good with a bow."

Catriona gave a light tsk of her tongue. "But your English accent would give ye away."

"Och, bloody Sassenachs," Samuel said, mocking the Scots' brogue.

"A noble effort, Sir Samuel." Catriona giggled and took another sip of the savory stew.

"Have you thought more about how you will entice your relations to help get rid of the English?"

The sudden change in subject caused Catriona to lose her smile. She chewed her lip. Could she trust Samuel? She wasn't entirely certain she could, but just as she'd had no choice in trusting him as her companion, she might as well at least give him some of the truth.

"My cousin is married to a laird who is involved with… our guardian. I think they will help me. At least, I hope they will."

Samuel's eyes widened. "Our guardian?"

"The Guardian of Scotland," Catriona whispered hoping their hosts weren't listening too keenly. If they caught anything and took it out of context, instead of spending the night warm beneath a roof, they'd be out in the snow again—that is if their hosts even let them make it past the door alive.

Samuel flicked his gaze toward the family behind Catriona, then mouthed, "William Wallace?"

She nodded, but the look that slowly closed over Samuel's face—guarded, entirely too interested—sent a shiver of fear racing through her. Had she said too much?

"I should like to meet him," Samuel murmured.

"Why?" she asked, suddenly on the defensive for her fellow countrymen.

Samuel shrugged, feigning disinterest, but it was far different from the earlier spark in his eyes. "Because he is a legend among men."

She took a sip of soup and then stared him straight in the eyes when she whispered, "And the single most wanted enemy of England."

Samuel locked his gaze on hers, wiping all expression from his features. "That is not why I want to meet him."

Was he lying? She studied his eyes. Blue as the sky, it seemed that she could search forever within them before she found anything remotely evil. And yet, he was her enemy. And she his. And she was leading him directly to the man he most likely had been trained to kill on sight.

"He will be surrounded by an army," Catriona warned. "Put your ambitions for rising in the ranks of Longshanks' army behind ye, Sassenach, else ye find your head rolling beside your feet."

Samuel chuckled. "Ye have an uncanny knack of issuing threats that could make any man quake, Catriona, but I have to wonder"—he leaned closer so his forehead was nearly on hers and his breath tickling her cheek—"what would you do if put to the test?"

Catriona pondered Samuel's question. What would she do if put to the test? She tried to keep the smile from her face, but the corners of her mouth twitched. She knew exactly what she would do.

Chapter Eight

THE following morning Samuel begrudgingly woke with a screaming headache—most likely from the lack of sleep. He'd tossed and turned in the rank room off the side of the croft—one time earning a kick from some animal, he wasn't quite sure which. But oddly, right now, he felt warm, and... aroused. The lack of windows made the room dark, but judging from the curvy female form beneath his arm and thigh, he had company. His cock was hard and pulsing as it pressed against rounded buttocks.

Ballocks! He stiffened, suddenly very concerned. Who was it? The mistress of the house would be bad, but even worse was Catriona.

He tried to tug his arm gently from beneath the head full of soft locks and failed miserably, hearing the thud as her skull hit the ground.

"Ouch!" 'Twas Catriona. She shifted beside him, sitting up.

Satan's curse!

He must have slept harder than he thought to have not felt her slide under his blanket and mold her delectable body to his. He was fully awake now and light from the main room shifted into this darker one. Catriona swiped her hand through her hair and stared up at him accusingly.

"What the hell are you doing in here?" he asked, leaping to his feet and checking to make sure he was wearing his clothes. Fully dressed, thank the saints.

Though, his body was reacting before his brain could tame it, growing harder still. The power of his desire for her was somewhat startling. He turned his back, lighting a candle he'd found the night before and pretending to prepare the horses so she wouldn't see the ever increasing bulge.

"I—" But she didn't say anything else, just huffed a breath.

Rustling sounded from behind, and then she was walking past him with another horse blanket and saddle.

She glanced up at him with sheepish eyes, crimson coloring her cheeks.

"What is it?" he asked, peering through the open door to the main room. But all he could think about was the way she'd felt in his arms, soft, silky, warm, curves in all the right places.

Catriona let out a harsh breath. "The giant and his wife... They were..." Her cheeks colored even more.

A few more minutes of him being half asleep and he might have done the same thing to her.

Samuel restrained himself from laughing, but a brief bursting chuckle left his mouth. "So you thought it best to cuddle up with me?" he teased, also relieved that he had woken up in time before his unconscious mind had taken the action his cock had desired.

Her mouth fell open, obviously reading more into what he'd said than he intended. Or had he intended it? Watching the emotions cross over her face was very entertaining, especially after the tease she'd given him upon waking.

"Certainly not. I only preferred not to hear the two of them carrying on beneath their blanket."

Samuel grinned and winked. "I don't blame you. Been plenty of times I've been in that same situation. Nearly was this morning."

Her mouth fell open. "In your dreams, Sassenach."

"Aye." He left it at that, because as much as he was supposed to hate her for being a Scot, he found her utterly enticing and altogether intriguing.

She glanced at him from over the back of her mount and looked as though she wanted to ask him a question, but then ducked her head and the moment was lost. Damn, but he wanted to ask what she would say. Wanted to know if she'd felt heat coursing through her veins when he'd held her. Wanted to know if she'd like to try again... Oh, devil's cock but he couldn't be thinking that way. They had several more days' travel—if not a fortnight—that they'd be alone together.

"Would ye mind terribly if we got on our way?" Her voice came out throaty, harsh. The sound of it did things to his mind and body, pushing him almost to the brink of his limits.

Samuel wanted to kiss her, wanted to press her up against the wall as he'd done at the castle, so he could feel her heart beat beneath his, but instead he cleared his throat. "Not at all. Have you looked outside?"

She shook her head, tending to her horse.

"I'll go and check then." The byre had no windows—a poor decision considering the smell of the muck on the floor. No doubt when he and Catriona left, they'd both need a good scrubbing to get the scent of animal dung off their clothes.

He tiptoed into the main room. All still slept save the woman who stirred porridge in the pot. She glanced at him, her eyes widening, and she looked ready to scream.

"We'll be leaving in a moment; I just wanted to get a peek out your window."

She closed her mouth and nodded.

Samuel opened the shutter. Outside, the ground was covered in a thick layer of white and the limbs sparkled with ice, but the sky was clear of clouds and the sun just beginning to burst on the horizon. Looked to be frigid, but at least the storm had passed.

"The horses are ready," Catriona whispered beside him. "It stopped snowing."

Samuel nodded. "We'll ride until it's dark, and look for shelter along the way."

She glanced up at him sideways, and nodded. "Aye, we will." There was something odd in her face, the way she said it that made him uncomfortable. Just where was she taking him? Why did he suddenly feel as though he was no longer the one deciding their destination?

Catriona turned to their host and said, "Thank ye so much for your hospitality. We'll be on our way now."

"Care for some porridge before ye leave?"

"Aye," Samuel said quickly before Catriona could deny the woman's offer. He glanced down at his guide and said, "We've a long way to go today. 'Twould be good to leave with a full belly."

She chewed her lip and fidgeted, but in the end nodded and accepted the bowl the woman handed her. They ate quickly as the family rose and slowly began their own morning duties. Not a half-hour later, Samuel and Catriona had led their horses outside and were preparing to depart. The family had firmly closed the door behind them, leaving Samuel to wonder at their own standings within their country.

"We need to move," Catriona said, her breath forming small steam clouds as she spoke. It was frigid, but the wind did not blow. Much better traveling conditions. "I've a terrible feeling in my bones that the English will soon know we were here."

The way she said, the English, made it sound almost like she no longer lumped him in with his own people. For some ungodly reason, that pleased him. He didn't want her to think of him with as much disdain as she thought of the rest of his countrymen.

"Lead the way," he said, "for we are both in trouble should the English catch up with us."

Catriona glanced around, perhaps taking in the direction of where they'd come from in the dark, and then veered her horse to the right. "If we cross through the border between McNab and MacLaren land, we'll be safe from the Campbells for a while."

Samuel knew nothing of the names, but trusted she wouldn't want to put herself in danger, and so he followed her along the wooded road. Their horses, having been well rested, warmed and fed, easily trotted on the course, kicking up tufts of snow.

"What is the name of your relation from whom we are going to visit?"

"Visit?" The high pitch of her voice gave away her nerves.

"Where are we headed?" Samuel said in a more stern voice.

Catriona's shoulders slumped briefly before she straightened them again. "We are headed to Sutherland, as ye requested."

Samuel reached out, realizing too late that he was touching her when he'd promised that he would never do so again. But the lass had curled up beside him the night before; she could handle his hand at her elbow.

"There is something you aren't telling me."

She glanced down at his hand on her elbow, but made no move to pull away; instead, she slowed her horse as though she wanted him to continue touching her.

"Everyone has their secrets." A slight curve lifted the side of her lip. "And I am part of that group. But, ye must trust that in this, I will help ye get your sisters back, and I do pray that no harm has come to them."

"As do I." Samuel couldn't bear to even think about what his sisters might be going through at that very moment.

"Samuel," she said softly. "I am aware that there are men of Scottish descent who are just as cruel as men like Sir Geoffrey."

She glanced back at him, brows furrowed and he wanted to ask how she knew that, for it seemed that she had her own tales to tell.

"When I say I'll pray for your sisters, I do not lie, Samuel. Ye'll have to trust me on our journey."

Samuel studied her profile, taking in her creamy complexion with a touch of rouge on her high cheekbones. She might be beautiful, but she was also hiding something. And intuition told him that she was indeed not headed to Sutherland. "If 'tis all the same to you, my lady, I trust no one."

Catriona grunted. "Then I suppose we have more in common than I first thought." She clucked to her horse and hurried forward, an obvious move to deter him from further discussion.

Had crawling into his makeshift bed been a way to distract him? Confuse him upon waking into thinking of other things besides their mission so she could... What? He couldn't figure it out, but he was nearly certain she was up to something.

He'd let her have her way for the moment, but by the end of the day, he'd know exactly what it was this little Scottish wench was up to.

HE WAS ONTO HER.

But Catriona cared about her brother and her clan a lot more than she cared for Samuel's cause. They came first. Which meant she had to lie to him. And really, what did a little lie matter anyway? She had no loyalties to Samuel other than her promise to help him find his sisters, which, with her change of plans, there was still a fairly good chance she would.

She was normally a very good liar, but this English knight always seemed to see right through her.

They rode for the next several hours in silence, crossing quietly between the two clans' lands with only two incidents where they had to stop and lay low until scouts passed. It was cold outside, but the cloak and blanket she'd been given did keep her body mostly warm. She wasn't as cold as she'd been the day before in the storm. A night before the fire had dried her clothing. However, her boots were still slightly damp and the cold of the day only made them colder. She kept her toes wiggling to keep them from freezing right off.

Only a couple more hours and they could begin looking for shelter for the night. The horse she rode was already starting to slow down. She took her pace down to a walk to give the animal a bit of rest.

And then she saw it. The huge oak tree that spanned six feet in diameter. The way the seed had split hundreds of years earlier created two trees that grew as one. 'Twas named the Fairy Tree—or at least that's what she'd been told—of Handsel Gleann. The patterns of the swirling bark looked like a fairy had carved a door that led into a magical realm. The tree was also directly in the center of a circle of stones. A sacred ground. She'd never forget seeing this tree and stones on her last journey north, the way it made her blood tingle with ethereal power—nor that a warm spring was a short hike up the crag behind it.

"Shall we stop to water the horses?" Catriona asked, finding it hard to hide the excitement from her voice. Within a few minutes, she could be dipping her toes into a heavenly pool of warm water.

Samuel was staring in amazement at the circle and tree, and she wondered if her own face had looked much the same upon first seeing such an impressive sight.

Finally, he glanced over at her. "Is there a creek nearby?"

Catriona cocked her head. "'Haps something a little warmer."

Chapter Nine

"WARMER?" The way Samuel cocked his eyebrow, his gaze flowing up and down the length of her body had Catriona's memory bringing vividly to the forefront the way she'd woken that morning.

Curling up in his arms had not been her intention. In fact, when she'd fallen asleep, there had been a good foot of distance between them, but it appeared that one or both of them had unconsciously pushed past the invisible boundary she'd set until they were so close they touched—and then his arm had wrapped around her middle. Her behind was pressed tight to the front of his body and she could feel every, single, inch of him. Thighs to thighs. Back to chest. Even their breathing had been in unison.

And just as she'd realized exactly how they were positioned, he'd yanked his arm out and her head had hit the ground. Thank goodness it hadn't hit that hard, else she'd still have a headache from it.

She could feel her face heating again, but she pushed past her embarrassment and smiled warmly. "Aye, Sassenach. There is a warm spring beyond Handsel Gleann that is calling to me."

Samuel still looked skeptical. He kept raking his gaze over her as if

"

trying to read her mind. "I've heard of such a thing, but never seen one with my own eyes."

Catriona kept her face purposely blank of any emotion or reaction —at least that was what she hoped. "'Tis magical."

"So you do know where you're going," he murmured, followed by a short laugh.

"Did ye think I was leading ye on a merry jaunt with no end?"

He shrugged. "I admit to the thought crossing my mind."

"For shame, English, ye should have a little faith."

"But as we discussed before, I trust no one."

Catriona pursed her lips. "Aye, and neither do I." She glanced over at him, saw that Samuel was studying her, and felt her face heat all the more. Why was it this man made her feel this way? Made her think thoughts that had no place in her mind? She was already a ruined woman—not that anyone knew, but she and her brother. And considering it had not been of her choosing, Gregor had promised to keep the knowledge from anyone else. "Do ye trust me enough to follow me up the hill and see if the hot spring truly exists?"

"As cold as my toes are, I'd be willing to follow you if you said there was a fire lit by a dragon."

Catriona let out a little laugh. "We have only fairies here, ye can keep your dragons."

Samuel winked. "Which is mightier?"

"I'm surprised ye wouldn't think a dragon, sir," she said, steering her horse around the tall stones and then up the slippery slope behind them.

"Fairies have magic."

"And dragons have fire." Her horse slipped on the slushy hill and she gripped tight to the reins. "Might be better to walk them up." She dismounted and started to climb, leading the horse, with Samuel doing the same behind her.

"Fire is not always more potent than magic," Samuel called.

"True. If the two were to mix, then we'd have real trouble."

"I've seen it mix before." Samuel was walking beside her now, staring at her the way he had that morning, when her body had stirred molten hot and she'd felt the evidence of his arousal against her back.

"When?"

They crested the hill and for a moment they both stilled in silence at the sight of the steaming pool set in the icy backdrop. A wall of rock rose up behind the pool, and trees surrounded them like a wall, as though nature wished for whoever would enjoy this spot to have privacy.

"Saints," Samuel breathed out.

"Aye, English." Catriona tied her horse loosely to a tree so it could nuzzle its way through the snow to grass.

"Will we not freeze to death?" he asked.

"Nay. Ye dinna wear your clothes into the pool." Oh, lord, but she hadn't thought about the fact that she'd have to get naked to enjoy the spring. When she'd been before, the women had stripped down to their chemises while the men turned their backs, but it had also been the middle of summer and so a little wet undergarment hadn't bothered them at all. In the middle of winter, 'twould be another story. "We can just dip our toes in." Letting him see her bare feet, ankles and calves wouldn't be the end of the world, especially not after the way he'd touched her that morning. In fact, a spark of something hot whizzed its way through her veins.

"Ah, yes, we'll not submerge fully."

"Right," she said.

Catriona approached the pool, found a smooth rock and used the back of her cloak to dust off the snow that sat atop it, then she took a seat, and started to unlace her boots.

"Will ye not join me?" she asked, flicking her gaze back at Samuel who simply stared at her.

Hunger flared momentarily in his eyes. "Haps I should keep watch while ye warm your feet."

Catriona cocked her head and listened to the sounds around them. Nothing. She beckoned him forward. "Nonsense. I hear no one nearby. Come dip your toes and then we'll be on our way."

Samuel stared at her a moment longer, indecision in his stance and expression. But as she slipped off her second boot, he tied his horse to a tree near hers then approached.

Catriona let out a moan as she slipped her frozen toes into the pool. The pleasure and pain of the hot liquid against her cold skin was enough to catch her breath. It felt so damn good.

"Hurry, Samuel, this is decadent," she murmured, eyes closed and head bent backward, arms bracing her against the cool rock.

Opening her eyes, she saw him standing over her, looking down with amusement.

"That good?" he asked.

Catriona laughed. "Aye."

She patted the space on the rock beside her and he took a seat—close enough that his hip touched hers and a shiver of another kind wound its way through her. Every time he was near her, her body reacted with need. She tried to ignore it. Tried to push it away. But it always found its way back, winding around her spine and making her limbs sing.

Samuel made quick work of removing his boots and hose, then he too let out a moan as the warmth of the spring slid over his skin.

"That is truly magnificent," he said.

"Are ye not glad I said we should stop?"

"Eternally," he said, leaning over a moment to bump his shoulder against hers.

She wiggled her toes beneath the water and slowly glided her legs back and forth, wishing she could just jump right in and dunk all the way under. As she brought her foot back toward her, her heel bumped against Samuel's toes.

"Sorry," she murmured, turning to look at him sheepishly.

"Nothing to apologize for." His gaze locked on hers as his toes skimmed slowly up the side of her foot.

The move was deliberate.

Warmth cascaded over her as though she had jumped into the pool. What they were doing was reckless. But at that moment, she didn't care. Catriona slid her own foot against his, and then he did the same, until their feet were tangled and tickling against one another.

"My lady," Samuel started, his voice gruff.

"Aye?" she asked, though she was completely distracted by his lips and how much she wished to kiss him.

"May I…" He glanced away and his feet stilled.

"May ye what?" she asked.

Samuel blew out a harsh breath, and drew closer to her, his hand cupping her cheek, his thumb stroking her jaw. "What is it about you, Catriona?" He spoke whisper-soft and it felt like each syllable caressed every part of her.

"I dinna know what ye mean," she said, but she did know. She had a very good idea because she felt the same thing. A confusing need to be with him, for him to like her, for him to touch her and kiss her.

"From the moment I saw you standing tall before Geoffrey and his crew, not allowing the man to brow beat you as he wanted, I was… intrigued." Samuel shook his head, drawing even closer. Her cheek burned where his hand rested, where his thumb stroked. "And every moment that has passed since, my curiosity has only grown. You fascinate me."

"Aye," she murmured, having had much the same problem.

And then his lips were brushing over hers. Catriona's eyes slid shut. She breathed in his woodsy, spicy scent. Melted against the warmth of his mouth. Sank against him. She caught his tunic in her hand, holding on for dear life as her body seemed to float to some other part of the woods or sky, she wasn't sure.

She sighed and kissed him back. The first to touch the tip of her tongue to his lips, she smiled when Samuel let out an oath under his breath. Her one timid act was enough to unleash something within him, as he clasped the other side of her face, thumbs at her temples as he tipped her head and deepened their kiss. Beneath the water their feet tangled. On the rock their hips and thighs were crushed side by side. Her breasts pushed against his hard chest. Tongues twined. Soft moans escaped. She wrapped her arms around his waist and held tight to the onslaught of sensations.

Samuel's hand slid from her face to her ribs, his fingers gently caressing just beneath her breasts. Her nipples tightened and fire ignited in her core. Was this what he meant when he was talking of magic and fire all in one?

Saints bones, she'd never been kissed like this before.

Aye, she'd done her share of kissing the stable hands and warriors before the one incident that changed her life—the seduction of the Campbell heir. Kissing came naturally to her. 'Twas an act she quite enjoyed, but never had she enjoyed it as much as she did now. And mayhap she should have been scared, given the way kissing in the past had turned out, but she wasn't. Not with Samuel. He made her feel safe. With him, she felt she could be herself, that she could let down her guard.

And, like a thunderclap, she realized that she trusted Samuel. Trusted him with every fiber of her being.

How long had it been since she'd trusted someone? Too long.

Was it a trick? A trick of her mind because he kissed so well? Because he could command her body with a gaze? The most terrifying part of it all was she didn't think that was it. There was something deeper, something that struck a chord in her soul. She wasn't ready for that.

Catriona pressed her hands against the hardened, sculpted muscles of his chest and gave a little push. Samuel halted their kiss at once, his forehead pressed to hers for a moment as their rapid breaths mingled, and then he pulled away.

"I'm sorry," he said. "I should not have taken such liberties with you."

Catriona smiled, though inside, her mind was at war with her feelings and desires. "Ye dinna need to be sorry. I wanted to kiss ye as much as ye wanted to kiss me."

Samuel shook his head. "I should not have. I promised at your castle that I would never do such a thing."

She locked her gaze on his, studying the way the icy blue color had warmed, reminding her of the pool beside them. "Unless I wanted ye to."

Samuel's eyes widened. "And did you?"

Slowly, Catriona nodded. "Aye. But now we must be away."

"Indeed, before we are come upon by fairies." Samuel's melodic voice had deepened, and was gravelly with some emotion that played right along the edges of her desire, tugging at some untamed part inside her.

"There is that." Catriona regrettably pulled her feet from the water and dried them on the hem of her gown before slipping on her hose and boots.

Samuel pulled on his hose and boots beside her in silence.

"What have we here? A Sassenach bastard and a traitor Scots bitch?"

Catriona whirled around to see three rough looking Highlanders standing between her and Samuel and their horses. They had their swords drawn, and leering smiles upon their hungry lips that made her skin crawl. She and Samuel had not heard the men approach. Too distracted by each other. This was all her fault. Why had she ever asked him to stop? They should have just kept on going and bypassed the outlaws all together.

Samuel stiffened beside her. How good was he at fighting? She had no clue. He must have some skill to have survived this far into his military career, and yet, was he skilled enough to thwart one or two Highlanders? She could take on one, perhaps the scrawniest, but at least it was something.

They both slowly stood. "Let me speak," she whispered to Samuel then turned to the threatening men. "We have no quarrel with ye," she started, holding her hands out to the side to show she was unarmed. "We'll just be on our way."

The men laughed, but the one in the middle, clearly the leader, stepped forward and said. "Unfortunately, we've a quarrel with ye, lass, and that stinking pile of shite standing beside ye."

She was afraid that would be their response. In this area, the people were bound to have been attacked by the English more than once, and there was no way they were going to let Samuel go, nor her, whom they believed to be a traitor. If the men had it their way, they'd see Samuel's throat slit, but they'd let her suffer. Rape her, beat her.

She shivered, her knees starting to knock, but she couldn't let her fears, or these men, take away her sense of power. Her sense of self.

"That is unfortunate, indeed," Catriona started, feigning bravery. She wasn't going down without a fight. "For ye'll have to dismiss any violent thoughts from your mind. We'll not be your prey today."

Chapter Ten

SAMUEL groaned inside. The lady was only goading the three brutes.

He'd known men like them before, having crossed paths with many in France, England and even a few in Scotland before they'd arrived at Buchanan. They wouldn't back down from a fight, not when a prize was within sight. Two horses, the chance to kill an Englishman and the opportunity to spread the thighs of one so delicious as Catriona was enough to make these men fight to the death.

Taking a deep breath, Samuel stepped in front of Catriona. "Your quarrel is not with the lady, but with me," he said, chest out, shoulders squared.

The men laughed, the leader going so far as to slap at his knee. "Ye're right, Sassenach, we're itching to slit your throat."

The way this man said Sassenach was infinitely less appealing than when Catriona said it. With her, it was almost a term of endearment.

A grin split Samuel's face. "Well, I'd be lying if I didn't say the feeling is mutual."

Catriona gasped. "What are ye doing?" she whispered under her breath. "Dinna goad them!"

Samuel didn't respond to her. These men didn't need to know how much he cared about her welfare in the outcome of this fight. This would not be a fair fight. Their weapons were crude, as were their manners. He'd taken on three skilled fighters in the past. Three dismal men would be exhausting but not too difficult. He slid his sword from his scabbard, the metal glinting in the sun that filtered through the trees.

"Who will be the first among you to die?" He smiled with dangerous intent at his enemies.

"Samuel, nay," Catriona said beside him, placing a hand on his arm as though to stop him.

Without taking his eyes from the men who would likely strike if he did, Samuel said, "Step back toward the trees, lass. I'll not let them lay a finger on you. I promised to keep you safe if you helped me and I intend to honor that vow."

"But ye canna—" she started, then stopped when Samuel did look at her for a fleeting moment.

"Go," he said, his eyes pleading.

She nodded resolutely, and if he had more time to think on it, he might try to guess what the pinched turn of her lips meant, but as she backed away, the brutes surrounded him, circling with their weapons drawn. Two men held swords and the third brandished a long dagger in each of his meaty fists. From the looks of it, they intended to fight him off at once. He couldn't say he was surprised.

Samuel took a deep breath and bent his head from side to side, cracking the tension from his muscles.

He kept his eyes on the leader, though keen to the movements of the men who flanked him.

"Anytime now," he goaded.

Sword up, he grabbed a dagger from his hip since he was without his shield which was inconveniently still upon his horse with his helmet.

The leader lashed forward, his sword coming close, but not close enough before Samuel blocked with a strike of his own. This man may be a decent fighter, but not more so than himself. The leader launched an attack again, which Samuel checked. His two men each leapt forward when their leader jumped back, but Samuel was ready for them. He ducked down, and swiveled on his heel slicing first one and then the second across the backs of their knees with his dagger, then whirled again and sliced across the tops of their thighs.

The two men howled, limping back a safe distance from Samuel's sword. Before he could stand, their leader was pouncing on him again, giving him a kick in the chest, which shook off his balance and nearly had him on his arse, except he'd practiced this many times with his men, and bending backward slightly, he pushed himself up with his palm. Without missing a breath, he parried against the leader, pushing him back and back until he was teetering near the edge of the hot spring.

"Have you had enough?" Samuel asked.

"I'll not have enough until your blood drenches the ground."

"You'll not be having it your way, today," Samuel said.

They continued to swing their swords, clashing in the quiet forest save for the sounds of their curses and the whimpers of the injured attackers.

Heavens above, he hoped that Catriona was safely hidden behind a tree—or better yet, upon her horse—and not seeing any of this. She seemed to be a tough woman, but women were so much gentler than men and should be protected.

A guttural growl from one of the thugs several feet away showed one of the attackers face down and a pretty dagger in his back. Catriona still stood behind the tree, but her stance looked as though she'd just thrown the dagger.

"Your bitch will pay for killing my man," the leader said, pushing harder with his sword, swinging haphazardly and violently.

Samuel blocked every attack, slicing here and there at the Scots maggot until he bled from gashes on his arms, chest and belly. And then finally, Samuel gave him a death blow that knocked the man into the hot spring, where he sank beneath its depths in a pool of watery red. What a shame to ruin such a beautiful and magical pool.

He turned to find Catriona, but saw her not. And then he heard her scream, and felt the pain as an arrow pierced through his hauberk, tunic, chainmail armor and into his chest.

Samuel glanced down at the shaft protruding from where his heart beat. He grabbed the wooden stave and yanked, but the blood pouring from the wound made it slippery. He broke it in half, leaving the arrow in his chest, and staggered forward.

"Catriona," he bellowed, but the sound came out muted, not quite a whisper.

The dead outlaw lay on the ground beside his bleeding friend who also had an arrow in his chest.

"Catriona," he said again.

But what he heard in answer was, "Magnus, no!" A cry so potent with heartache, he felt it clear inside his gut and down to his toes. 'Twas not the voice of his companion but of his sister.

"Arbella?" Samuel whirled in a circle, his feet sliding in the blood-reddened snow. Was his sister here? Or was she calling to him from the heavens?

He turned again, falling to his knees when his feet refused to work. "Oh, Catriona, I have failed you," he said. "Arbella, I'm coming now. I've failed you and Aliah. Forgive me."

And he fell backward, eyes directed toward the sky, where it went from grey to black.

HE WAS GOING TO DIE.

Catriona stared down at the prone bleeding body of Sir Samuel de Mowbray. The man who had saved her from her attackers, swept her up into a whirlwind of emotion and made her believe that maybe, just maybe, she could trust again. That a lifetime of loneliness was not her sentence.

But now he lay bleeding, an arrow protruding from his chest.

She was suddenly alarmed as the facts of what happened sank in. They were now surrounded by a new party of people. Had they been the one to shoot Samuel?

"What have ye done?" she asked the warrior who stood beside her, frowning down at Samuel.

"Samuel!" A beautiful blond—who spoke as an Englishwoman— dropped beside Samuel, grabbed onto his face and shook him gently. "Wake, brother! Wake up!"

Catriona was almost jealous until she realized who they must be— Magnus Sutherland and his wife Arbella, Samuel's sister. The woman did not appear to be too distressed; in fact the way she'd spoken to her husband showed she couldn't possibly be afraid of him. Was it conceivable that Samuel had it wrong? Had Arbella willingly gone into the arms of a Highlander?

"God's bones." Catriona slapped her hands to her face, disbelieving what she was seeing. How could they be here? "We were looking for ye."

"Me?" Arbella asked, then she whipped her gaze to her husband, her eyes and voice edging on hysteria. "You killed my brother!"

"Samuel asked me to help him find ye." Catriona's voice trailed off as her gaze fell back on the English knight. His pallor had faded and blood seeped through the liveried tunic in a darkened stain. "He saved me."

"He still breathes," Arbella said. "Though 'tis weak. I think the arrow just missed his heart, though this means nothing. He could still die."

"Get him on a horse. We're not that far from Blair Castle," Magnus ordered. "They'll have a healer there who can help him."

Two retainers leapt to the ground and lifted Samuel with Arbella fussing around him.

"Wait!" Catriona yelled, putting her hands out toward them. "Ye canna take him." If they were close to Blair, she'd take him there herself.

Arbella straightened her shoulders, a determined frown on her face. "He's my brother. We'll take him wherever I choose."

Catriona shook her head, her fingers tingling and her vision blurring with tears. She blinked them away, forcing herself to remain strong. "But how do I know ye are who ye say ye are? Ye're the ones who shot him!"

The retainers paused a moment before the horse as they tried to figure out the right position to put him on.

Arbella's face softened. "To be correct, 'twas my husband who shot him."

Husband... Arbella was not only stolen by the man, but married to him to. "Exactly. How can I, in good conscience, allow ye to take him with the man who shot him riding with ye. He may cloud your judgment and do further harm."

Arbella put her hands on her hips. "What is he to you?"

Catriona narrowed her eyes and took several steps toward Samuel. "He is..." Her voice trailed off. What was he to her? She was his guide. He was her savior. They were friends. They were... What? Their heated kiss made them more than just friends. And then words were flowing from her mouth before she could think of anything more plausible to say that would keep her with him, and allow her to make certain he remained safe. "He is my husband."

Everyone stilled, their eyes jerking toward Catriona. She felt the color drain from her own face, and then her body started to tremble. She locked her knees, squeezed her legs and stomach, clenched her fists, to keep the tremors from showing to all who stared at her.

"You are married?" Arbella asked, her voice faint, her hand clutching at her neck.

Catriona nodded, not trusting her voice to come out strong. Had she truly just claimed this man to be her husband in front of all these witnesses? If he were to claim the same thing, under Highland law, they would be truly wed. But he wouldn't and as soon as he came to, she would tell him what she did, and then he would let them know that she'd done it to protect him. They would all laugh about it later—if they were friends and not foe.

Though they were Highlanders, how was she to know if she could trust them? After all, Magnus Sutherland and his brother had married Englishwomen. Then again, everyone in their entire family was deeply entrenched in the war for Scottish freedom. If they could be trusted by the guardian of Scotland—William Wallace—and by the future king—Robert the Bruce—didn't that mean she could trust them, too?

It was all too much. She bit the inside of her cheek to keep the sob at the back of her throat from escaping.

"When?" Arbella asked.

Had his sister had any correspondence? Nay, she couldn't have, because Samuel had said he didn't know where they were.

"Not long," she answered, deciding that being vague was the best course of action for now.

"What is your name?" Magnus asked.

Catriona faced the fearsome dark warrior. His size and the power that he exuded reminded her of her brother Gregor. Which only made her sad, because she had no idea how he fared at the moment—was he even still alive?

Swallowing away her fear for her brother, she squared her shoulders. She had to stay strong for Gregor, she had to stay strong for Samuel. This wasn't about her. Everyone had to make sacrifices some time, and right now she was making hers. And it was only short term. "I am Lady Catriona Buchanan."

"Of Clan Buchanan?" Magnus asked. "Gregor's younger sister?"

She nodded, feeling her trembling ease somewhat. "Ye know him?"

"Oh, aye." The way he said it was as though Gregor had made a name for himself amongst the clans, and she couldn't help but wonder what exactly that was all about. "Ye're coming with us."

Chapter Eleven

RIPPLES of panic shuddered up and down Catriona's spine. Though she knew she'd done the right thing in order to protect Samuel, she was also terrified that she'd sealed her brother's and her clan's fate. The only thing she had on her side was that Blair was the castle she'd intended to take Samuel to without his knowledge.

Her distant cousin Myra lived at Blair Castle as her husband Daniel was laird and chief of Clan Murray. In a weird and twisted turn of fate, perhaps the attack had been a good thing—though if she could change the way it played out, she would not have let Samuel get shot with an arrow to the heart. It was a miracle he was still breathing.

Their horses clopped over the bridge to Blair and the gates were flung open as soon as the keeper saw Magnus' entourage.

Catriona searched the sea of faces within the courtyard but did not see her cousin. Well, at least she didn't recognize her. It had been many years since last she'd seen her, and then they'd both been girls.

A man approached Magnus and within seconds was shouting orders to his men. A swarm surrounded Samuel and then he was whisked into the castle. Not a minute later, while Catriona dismounted, a woman rushed from the main castle doors. This one, she did recognize as her cousin Myra.

Myra rushed to Arbella, wrapping her in her arms, and then when she lifted her gaze to Catriona, recognition dawned.

"Cousin!" She held out her hand to Catriona beckoning her forward. "Why are ye with the Sutherlands?"

Catriona cleared her throat, finding it hard to speak. "I am..." Zounds, could she go through with this? Lie to her own blood? "I am married to Samuel."

Myra's face went blank as she assessed Catriona. "I see." Then a smile split her face and she nodded. "Of course, ye are. Come, let us get inside where 'tis warm. Ye must be freezing from your journey."

They followed Myra through a dimly lit entryway and up a winding stair and then into a well-lit great hall. A blazing fire filled the hearth and wax candles melted down from the simple iron chandeliers that hung from the rafters.

"Ye've arrived just in time for supper," Myra said. "Have a seat by the hearth here and I'll see about getting you both chambers and extra settings at the table."

As Catriona sank her weary bones into a cushioned wood back chair before the hearth, a servant rushed forward with a cup of wine. She gladly took the drink and sipped at it as she extended her feet toward the hearth to soak in some of the heat.

"I'm going to see about Samuel," Arbella muttered and started to rush off.

"Wait," Catriona said, "I'm coming with ye."

Arbella looked as though she wanted to argue, but instead nodded. Catriona passed her wine to a servant and followed Arbella up the winding stairs to the next level where shouting echoed from one of the rooms.

"They must be removing the arrow," Arbella muttered.

The image that brought into Catriona's mind made her queasy, but she pushed forward, refusing to let her nerves control her. She had to remain strong for Samuel's sake. After making certain he was all right, she'd beg a word with Myra and ask her to request her husband's assistance in ridding Castle Buchanan of the English.

Upon entering the room, however, she lost all train of thought. Samuel lay spread out on the bed, a warrior at each of his wrists and ankles, holding him down as a healer worked to carefully remove the arrow. The woman looked more like an old crone, ready to cross over at any given moment. Her hair was a gray tangled mess and her skin had more creases than a dried plum.

Samuel writhed and cursed and then it was out, and he fell back against the bed, eyes closed, mouth slack.

"He's out cold," one of the warriors said.

They eased their hold on his extremities, but as soon as the healer began cleaning the wound, Samuel was awake again. This time his gaze searched out Magnus.

"You shot me! You bloody bastard! I'll kill you for this and for stealing my sister!"

Cool air rushed over Catriona's side as Arbella ran toward her brother. "Samuel, please. Magnus did not steal me. You must lie still or else the healer won't be able to help you."

"He didn't steal you away?" He glanced back at the formidable warrior. "You went with that arsehole willingly?"

The shock and disbelief in his voice made Catriona want to laugh, but she pressed her lips together.

Even near death, Samuel had a sense of humor.

Arbella smiled at her brother. "Aye, I did. And Aliah with her husband. But, I'm not too happy he shot you."

"You shot me! I'll kill you for this," Samuel began again, but mid-sentence the healer gave him something to sip and moments later he was asleep once more.

"Outta the way now, missus, or I'll not be able to sew him up before he wakes again."

Arbella complied, going to her husband's side where she quietly chided him, and it looked as though her husband groveled. The man would have a lot of groveling to do for shooting his own brother-by-marriage and nearly killing him.

All the time she'd been in the room, no one acknowledged her, and she inched closer to the bed, feeling like in this sea of strangers the only one she knew and trusted was at their mercy.

"All done now." The healer glanced up at Catriona. "Ye'll want to keep his wound clean. I'll put the dressing on, but watch how I do it. The wound was deep, and missed his heart by half an inch. Fever could still set in."

Catriona's belly did a little flip. Blood had always been her weakness. She watched the healer clean and pack the wound with a poultice and bandages, biting her lip the entire time to keep herself from fainting just as Samuel had.

"Can ye handle this, missus?"

"Aye," Catriona murmured.

"I'll be here to help," Arbella said.

"As will I," Myra called from the doorway. She had a tray of broth and cups of something. "When can he eat?"

"Best to let him rest for now. He didn't wake during the sewing which means the tincture I gave him worked, and it should last a few hours if not through the night. Just be sure to keep him cool should his skin begin to heat. I'll be on my way now, but should ye need anything, send one of the lads to get me and I'll be right back." She glowered at the tall man who'd first approached them in the courtyard—Daniel Murray judging by the way Myra had taken hold of his arm. "I'll be requiring twice the payment since he's a bloody Sassenach."

Daniel grinned. "Talk to Sutherland, he's the one who shot the bastard."

"My brother-by-marriage," Magnus grumbled, pulling coins from his sporran and handing them to the crone. "Thanks for your assistance."

The old woman grunted and then left in a scurry of weathered skirts and medicinal scents.

Arbella broke away from her husband and tugged a wooden chair from the corner to the side of the bed. "You should take the first watch, since he is your husband."

Catriona nodded numbly. Her legs barely held her as she walked around the side of the bed. She braced her hands on the arms and lowered herself into the chair.

"We'll leave you both alone for a little while," Arbella said.

Catriona glanced up at the beautiful woman, taking note of the pained look in her expression. She didn't want to leave her brother, and Catriona could completely empathize with her pain since she hadn't wanted to leave her brother either, but before she could tell her to stay, Myra was whisking Arbella out of the room with a promise to have a meal sent up.

When the door closed leaving her alone with the man she'd known but a few days and had to pretend she was married to, panic once more filled her chest.

"Ye'll not believe what I did," she said to his prone body. She studied his closed eyes, lashes fanned over sun-kissed broad cheeks. His chest moved up and down in a slow, rhythmic pattern, much easier than it had before. "'Twas foolish of me, I know, but I could think of no other way to make certain ye were safe."

Samuel rolled his head to the side, eyes still closed and murmured something unintelligible.

"Ye'd better get well," she said, and then added, "for your sister's sake."

A quarter hour must have gone by when Samuel's hand twitched and he murmured. "Arbella..."

Catriona reached out and took his hand in hers. "She's here and well. Ye've nothing to worry over. Just need to heal now."

Sometime later, Catriona startled awake when a hand pressed to her shoulder. She sighed with relief to see 'twas Myra.

"Ye've had a lengthy journey." Myra said, her eyes soft with concern. She quietly picked up a stool and sat it beside Catriona. "Ye looked exhausted."

Catriona smiled and went to stretch, realizing her hand was still clutched in Samuel's.

Myra smiled at the sight. "I see ye both care for one another."

How could she answer that? Aye, she cared for Samuel, but... Her heart thudded against her ribs. She cared for him more than she realized. More than she wanted to, for soon they would have to part ways. This farce she'd created would end, and her cousin would resent her.

"He saved me," Catriona started. Now or never was the time to get assistance for her brother and clan. "He was in the English regiment that attacked Buchanan."

Myra's eyes widened, but she said nothing.

She explained about them going to the small chamber and how they'd escaped. That her brother was in danger. But instead of speaking about the crofters they'd spend the night with, she told a different version—of a small kirk where they'd sought refuge and married in secret before heading north to seek the help of Daniel Murray in saving her brother and clan.

"Zounds but ye've been through a lot." Myra stood. "We shan't waste another moment. I will tell Daniel at once."

"Thank ye so much," Catriona said, her voice catching on a sob. "Ye've no idea how much that means to me."

Myra bent and pulled Catriona into a hug. "Oh, but I do. Ye must recall the tale of my older brother Byron."

Catriona nodded, having forgotten that one of the reasons they'd gone north years before was because Myra's brother had been killed in a raid at their castle and Myra had been given no other choice but to escape with her brother's pregnant wife.

"I'm so sorry," Catriona whispered.

"Do nay be sorry, cousin. We will help ye, for I'd not want what happened to my brother to happen to yours." Myra gave her one more hug, then said, "Come eat what I've brought ye. I will go and speak with Daniel."

Catriona stood to sup on the stew and small ale Myra had set on a side table, thanking her cousin once more as she left. She'd just finished the last bite of stew when Arbella entered the room.

"The men will leave at first light," she said, her voice hoarse.

"For Buchanan?"

Arbella nodded, going to stand beside her brother and whisking a loose lock from his forehead.

"Myra told me what Samuel did for you," she said. "He was always so honorable."

Catriona stiffened. "Is, Arbella. He is honorable."

"That's what I meant." She sat in the chair Catriona had occupied. "I was so worried about him overseas. Not knowing if he lived or died. And then to see him for the first time in years and it be with an arrow in his chest." Her voice broke off on a sob, her hand clasping to her lips.

Catriona, wanting to comfort her, took the seat where Myra had been. "He's here now. Samuel is a fighter." She told Arbella of how he'd convinced the king to let him accompany Sir Geoffrey and that he'd secretly been on a mission of his own to find his sisters.

"And now he is a traitor to England?" Arbella asked, her mouth forming an O of alarm.

"Samuel is quick-witted. I'm certain he can remove any doubt from his king's mind of his allegiance."

"If that is what he chooses." Arbella nodded. "But how could that be the case with a Scottish wife?"

Catriona felt her face drain. She'd forgotten about that tiny detail. A dangerous slip to make.

"I see you'd not thought of that. Were you not planning to accompany him back to England?" Arbella eyed her with suspicion.

Catriona glanced at Samuel, her heart lurching to see him so weakened when she knew him only as strong. "We hadna gotten that far." She spoke the truth, for they'd only gotten as far as a steamy kiss and the hopes and dreams that came along with it. She sighed deeply. "All I knew was that he'd saved me, that I was helping him find his sisters. 'Twas a grand adventure, a whirlwind."

Arbella let out a short laugh. "As it is with all love. An adventure over many hills and valleys."

Love? Was that what this was that she felt?

Chapter Twelve

ONE moment Samuel was in the woods fighting outlaws and the next he was lying in bed, his chest giving off a subtle burn. From the weakened state of his muscles, he felt as though he'd been lying there for several days, maybe even a sennight.

He blinked open his eyes to see Catriona asleep in a chair beside him, her hand clutched in his. A small table beside the bed held the remains of what looked like a cloth, water and soap for bathing. He didn't feel as grimy as he should for having been in bed for so long. Must have had a bath. Had she been the one to bathe him?

Just how long had he been lying in this bed?

He blinked his eyes and with it came pieces of memory he had no recollection of encountering. Incredible pain. Confusion. His sister. Another woman he didn't recognize. But most blatant was a confession in the midst of delirium in which Catriona told him she'd lied to everyone, that she'd made up a story that they were married in order to keep him safe. Was it a fever induced dream? Or had she truly told everyone they were man and wife?

Samuel watched her sleep now, her face thinner than he remembered. Her hair a mess. And yet, she was still as beautiful as ever. He wouldn't mind being married to her. She'd been genuine with him from the start and he liked who she was. A feisty, honorable, driven, loyal woman. And rousing as hell.

He recalled vividly that kiss by the warm spring. How he wanted to relive it again.

Shifting in the bed, he gave her hand a little squeeze, and when she opened her eyes, he said, "Is it morning or night, wife?"

Catriona's eyes bolted open. "What?" she said, her lips pursing, pallor fading.

"Did you not say that I was your husband?"

She shook her head, but from the expression on her face, he was pretty certain she remembered it clearly. So, it hadn't been a dream, and that pleased him more than he was willing to admit.

"Ye've suffered a fever."

"Ah," he drawled out. "Is that why I feel addle-brained?"

She nodded mutely.

"And is that why I recall a grand tale of our escape and our marriage in a kirk?"

Now her cheeks flamed red, and she shifted uncomfortably in her chair.

The door to the chamber opened, and he continued with his story, knowing exactly what would happen.

"I remember it. You were so beautiful standing with me at the altar. Our hands clasped as we recited our vows. I took you to wife, vowing to keep you safe, to cherish you and you agreed to love and obey me for all of our days. In sickness and in health. We've weathered sickness now."

A sigh from the door made Samuel grin widely at Catriona who looked ready to faint.

"How long have I been asleep, my wife? And how long have you watched over me, praying for me to live so we might live out our days in happiness?"

"Nearly a fortnight," said the woman by the door.

Samuel turned his head, feigning shock at the intrusion. This was one of the women he recalled from his dreams. "And who might you be, an angel?"

She ducked her head and giggled, while Catriona yanked her hand away and gave a huff.

"Nay, sir, but Lady Myra, my husband is Laird Murray. This is our castle."

"My thanks for your hospitality," he said with sincerity.

"Ye're most welcome. Catriona is my cousin, and my husband is cousin to your sisters' husbands."

Samuel raised a brow. He did recall briefly that Arbella was happily married or so she confessed and that Aliah was, too, but he was still hoping to have heard wrong. "Sisters' husbands?"

"Aye, Magnus Sutherland is wed to Arbella and Blane Sutherland to Aliah."

He tried to sit up, but Catriona gently pushed him back down, handing him a minty tisane to sip. "Are they here? I must speak to them all."

Myra frowned and glanced at Catriona. "Ye haven't told him?"

His gaze flicked from one to the other and he frowned, setting the cup aside, suddenly fearful it was a sleeping drought. "Told me what?"

Catriona rolled her eyes back to his and frowned. "The men left about a sennight ago for Buchanan to get my castle back."

He nodded with relief. He hoped the Highlanders had beat Sir Geoffrey and his men into the ground and that it wasn't too late for Catriona's brother and her people. Already too many had been slaughtered. "That is good. I pray they find your brother well and that they give Geoffrey exactly what he deserves. But what of Arbella? Aliah?"

"Arbella should be here momentarily. She had a few things to tend to, and a missive was sent to Aliah and Blane the day after ye arrived," Catriona said. "They will be very pleased ye have woken."

Samuel nodded. "Not as pleased as I am."

The click of heels on the floorboards sounded as his sister, Arbella, entered the chamber. "I thought I heard the timber of a cranky knight's voice," she teased.

Samuel raised a brow. "I almost died and this is the love I get for it?" He held out his arms for his sister. She looked happier than he'd ever seen her.

"How is your wound?" Arbella said, coming forward to give him a gentle hug.

"It barely pains me."

"Your wife has taken very good care of you," Arbella said.

Samuel glanced at Catriona who had moved about six feet away and looked ready to bolt. He held out his hand to her, beckoning her forward, and knowing that she wouldn't dare leave with Myra and Arbella in the room.

Just as he'd hoped, she stepped forward and took his hand. Her fingers were cold and she trembled slightly. When he looked up at her she no longer looked as indignant as she had before, but frightened instead. She stared straight ahead at the wall, and he couldn't help but get the impression that she expected him to drop an ax on her head and oust her lie to everyone. He would never. Not on her life, and not on his.

What she didn't know was that he'd wanted so long to have someone to call his own. A woman to love and cherish. A woman just like Catriona. She'd claimed him, and now she was going to be stuck with him. That was—if she really wanted him. And he couldn't imagine she wouldn't. Wasn't that why she'd stayed behind when she could have returned with the men to get her castle back?

"She is a wonderful woman," Samuel said. "One I can't envision not having in my life." This time he spoke genuinely instead of teasing her as he had before.

Catriona turned her gaze on him, lips parting. He tugged on her hand. "Kiss me," he said.

She gave a slight shake of her head

Arbella and Myra giggled. "We'll leave the two of you alone." When they reached the door, Arbella said loud enough for them to hear, "Love in its beginning growth is such a merry journey that only grows stronger as the years pass."

The door clicked closed, and Samuel tugged on Catriona again. She tried to pull away, but he tugged her even harder until she tumbled down beside him with a squeak.

"There you go," he murmured, nuzzling against her neck. She

smelled of flowers and something distinctly her own. He buried his face in her hair and sucked in a deep breath.

"What are ye doing?" she asked.

"I'm going to kiss my wife," he murmured.

She stilled. "But I'm not your wife and ye well know it."

Samuel chuckled. "Ah, but I beg to differ. Did you not claim it? And did I not also claim it? Isn't that the way of the Highlands? Who is to say otherwise?"

She tried halfheartedly to pull away. "The Lord and the priest who doesn't exist."

"Well, if he does not exist, then how can he say otherwise? And as for the Lord, we can make it right, we'll go to the kirk right now."

"What?" She felt his forehead. "Ye must still suffer a fever."

Samuel snaked his arms around her waist, ignoring the dull ache in his chest. "I only suffer from need, lass. I want you to be my wife. I will gladly take this gift you offer."

"Only because ye want to kiss me."

"Nay. Well, aye, I do want to kiss you, but that is not why I want to marry you." He stroked a hand up her back. She shivered against him, and just that subtle reaction brought an immense response from his own body. All the blood rushed from his extremities and straight to his groin. And it was at that moment he realized beneath the blanket, he was nude. He let out a groan. 'Twas as if the fates were setting him up. But he was getting ahead of himself. Words and vows first.

"Why do ye want to marry me?" Catriona propped up on her elbow to study his face. "Ye're an Englishman, and ye hate the Scots."

"Not so. I've only met three I disliked immensely and I dispatched them."

"Well, ye canna dispatch of everyone ye dislike immensely, though I agree in the case of the three of whom ye speak."

Samuel grinned. "Does that mean ye'll marry me?"

"Ye still haven't told me why I should."

He wrapped a tendril of her hair around his finger, marveling at the softness. "Because, you fascinate me. I want to spend the rest of my life seeing what you'll do next. Because even though I've not known you long, I know you well enough to tell when you're scared, worried, embarrassed or that you want me to kiss you. Because I think I fell in love with you the moment I watched you stand up to that arsehole Geoffrey and I want to stand beside you when you tell every bastard you come across to bugger off. You stayed when you didn't have to. Catriona, tell me that means something and that I'm not just delirious with the magic of your enchantment."

"It means something," she whispered, inching closer so that she could trace his jawline with her finger. "I've never trusted another like I do ye. Ye've kept me safe, cared for me, were tender with me. And when we speak, I feel like ye're the only one who understands me. And this whole time"—her voice cracked—"when I thought ye might not wake, my heart ached. I realized I loved ye and that though I'd cooked up this scheme of our marriage, I wanted it to be real. I was terrified that when ye woke it would all be over."

Samuel's chest swelled with joy and love. "And now I've woken."

"And it's not over?"

"Not ever." He tilted her chin with his fingertips and pressed his lips to hers, savoring the softness.

Chapter Thirteen

CATRIONA eagerly kissed Samuel back, floating in the cloud of hope and the thrill of desire that thrummed through her veins.

Once more, he'd swept her up in his magic. A place she never wanted to descend from. Never in her wildest dreams or nightmares would she have thought she'd be lying in bed with a Sassenach, letting him stroke his hands over her back, her lips on his. And even if the thought had ever pierced her mind, it wasn't as delicious and pleasant as this. Samuel knew just the way to touch his tongue to hers, the right amount of pressure to massage the muscles along her spine until she arched her back in pleasure, and just the slightest soft brush of his lips over hers to make her entire body tremble.

The one and only other time she'd been with a man had been horrible. Her brother had been thinking of entering her into a contract for marriage with the man—a son of the Campbell chief. The young man had been so determined for the contract to go through that he'd seduced her with pretty words and then betrayed her—leaving her no longer a virgin. When her brother had changed her mind, she'd been both relieved and devastated. She'd thanked God every day when her monthly finally came.

Though she was no longer a virgin, at least she'd not born a child out of wedlock or been forced to marry the imbecile. But either way, it was a mar on her reputation that she needed to confess to this man who wished her to be his wife.

"Samuel," she murmured against his lips. "There is something I have to tell ye."

He slid his lips over her jawline to tease the lobe of her ear with his tongue. "Anything."

Tremors snaked over her and she leaned in closer, wanting to feel that again. He was driving her to distraction with his tongue.

"I am not... pure."

"None of us are pure, love." He said it so easily, he must not know of what she spoke.

"Nay, ye dinna understand. I have been... compromised." She closed her eyes, refusing to look at him. Her cheeks heated and she waited for the ridicules he was certain to toss at her.

Samuel stilled his movements, clasped his hands to either side of her face. "Look at me, Catriona."

She shook her head. "Just tell me to leave and I will."

"How could you say that?" His voice sounded hurt, prompting her to open her eyes. "I would never ask you to leave. Whether you are a virgin or not does not concern me, I know you are an honorable woman. But I must know one thing—were you raped? Was he an English knight?"

Wide-eyed with shock, she stared down into Samuel's blue eyes. He never ceased to amaze her. "Nay. Nay, he was Scottish and he didna rape me. He used me."

"Oh, love"—he stroked her cheek—"I'm so sorry."

Catriona shook her head. "Ye dinna need to be sorry. I was naïve and I should have seen him for what he was."

"I will never use you." His voice was filled with conviction.

She locked her gaze on his, admiring the way his eyes changed color once more, a deeper blue with passion. "I know."

He searched her gaze and threaded his fingers in hers. "I love you with every fiber of my being."

"I love ye, too, Samuel. I love ye so much." She squeezed his hand tight, half-expecting to wake from a dream.

"I want to make love to you. I want to show you what it is to be loved, cherished."

She glanced down at the bandaging on his chest. He had healed so well, but it had only been a fortnight. Was that enough time? "But your injury."

He shrugged, a wicked grin covering his lips. "Ah, 'tis nothing but a flesh wound now."

Catriona raised her brows, feeling compelled to give him a dose of reality, for she truly did not want him to be injured further. "Ye almost died."

"And now I feel more alive than ever." He brought her fingers to his lips and kissed every knuckle, the warmth of his breath making her shiver with anticipation. Every place he touched burned with need.

She pulled their joined hands to her own lips and kissed him as he'd done to her. "I'm so grateful that ye weren't taken away from me."

Samuel closed his eyes, and blew out a jagged breath. She loved that she could make him feel the same way he made her feel.

"I'm grateful you forced them to bring you to the castle," he said.

"Well, it wasn't exactly forced." She grinned and winked.

Samuel chuckled. "Ye're a clever woman."

"I'm just glad it worked."

He tugged her closer, resting his lips on hers once more, a tender exploration of her mouth. She melted against him, breathing in the clean scent of his skin. Once, she'd looked at his lips and wanted to know what it felt like to kiss him and now she knew. It was heavenly and she never wanted to stop.

Samuel slid his hands over her ribs and down to her hips, swirling circles and heating her flesh.

"Will you bar the door, love?" he whispered. "I don't want any interruptions, and this is not going to be quick. I want to savor every inch of you."

Catriona shivered. "Aye."

She started to slide off the bed, her feet touching the floor, but he leaned up on his elbow, and captured the back of her neck, pulling her in for another heated kiss. She straightened her legs to keep her knees from buckling as she grew dizzy with excitement and desire.

With one last nibble of her lips he let her go, and she practically ran to bar the door, but when she turned around and saw him lying there, lids hooded, eyes hazy with need, and a smile on his lips that made her quiver, she stilled. It was shocking how much she trusted him, loved him and how much she realized he wanted her, loved her.

She was going to marry this man. For all intents and purposes, they were already man and wife. Catriona took a few steps forward and stilled again. She wanted to watch the heady expression on his face deepen. Wanted to undress before him, to tease him, too. Long ago, after her encounter with the Campbell boor, she'd made a promise to herself that if she ever did find a man who actually wanted her for her and not for what could be gained by their union, that she would give herself to him wholly. And right now, in this chamber, that was exactly what she was going to do.

She slipped her fingers into the roped belt at her waist and slowly untied the knot, letting the fabric fall to the ground. Then she lifted her gown up over her head, feeling the whoosh of cold air against her thin chemise.

"Come closer." Samuel's voice had deepened and was gravelly with need.

Catriona shook her head, lifted her foot and placed it on a stool, aware that her chemise had hiked up to expose her calves and knees. She unlaced one boot and kicked it off, and watched Samuel's eyes darken as she slowly unrolled her hose. He leaned up further on his elbows to watch.

"You're a vixen, you know that? Is this a dream? When will I wake?"

"This is no dream, husband. This is only the beginning." Zounds, but where had that come from? One moment she'd been afraid he'd toss her out on her ear, and the next she'd become a wild seductress.

A sensual groan issued from his lips, causing her belly to quiver and liquid heat to pool between her thighs. She loved the power she possessed to make him want her, but at the same time, the way her body reacted in turn was stunning.

She lifted her foot to remove her other boot, and unroll her hose.

In the time she'd glanced down, Samuel had managed to climb from the bed and was stalking—naked—toward her like a wild animal to his prey. She shivered, liking the way his gaze raked over her. And liking even more the image of his nude form—he could have been carved from stone. Muscles rippled with every move. The white linen bandage was still in place covering his wound. A splash of blond hair touched his chest, and another between his hips. But what she couldn't take her eyes off of was the thickness of his shaft jutting toward her. Her mouth fell open as blood pumped a rapid pace through her veins. Her nipples tightened. Between her thighs tingled and she was suddenly hungry, thirsty, starving and it wasn't for food. It was an overwhelming yearning for him. To have his body on hers. To have him slide inside her and take ownership. To give herself to him for all eternity.

And then he was a breath away from her, the heat of his body reaching out and enveloping her. She sucked in deep.

"I couldn't let you have all the fun," he murmured, wrapping his arms around her. He pulled her taut to him, hands splayed on her back and his lips captured hers in a ravishing kiss.

She wanted to protest, afraid that he would only end up hurting himself, but of the two of them, he was steadier on his feet than she was. Catriona slid her hands around his trim waist and clutched his muscled back. The hardness of his arousal pressed hotly against her pelvis, and she wanted to wrench the chemise from her body to feel his heated flesh against her own.

Samuel must have wanted the same thing, because a moment later the fabric was gone and her chest was crashing hot against his. Their mouths were a frenzy of passion. Hands touching, stroking. He cupped her breast, and his thumb brushed over her nipple. She arched her back, hips tilting up into his. Her nails dug into the flesh of his back.

He cupped her buttocks, massaging the muscle. The length of his turgid flesh probed against the apex of her thighs.

"This is so different," she panted.

"Tell me," Samuel said, dipping to flick his tongue over her nipple.

"So... passionate. I feel..."

"What do you feel?" He drew her nipple into his mouth.

"Hot."

He kissed over her ribs and down the side of her body to her hip, and then over her belly to her navel. His tongue swirled around the edges and she gasped.

"And now?" he asked.

"Tingly."

She clung to him, afraid she was going to fall over. She swayed on her feet as Samuel paid equal attention to her other breast, while caressing over her thighs, and then one finger slid along the slickened folds of her sex, and Catriona's knees buckled. She cried out in both shock and pleasure. It had not felt this way her first time. That had been hurried, messy and painful. This was... She couldn't even describe it, other than to say she felt better than when she'd drunk heady wine. Better than what she expected heaven to feel like.

And then she knew for certain she was in heaven when he breathed hotly over her sex, and flicked his tongue over the sensitive folds.

"How does this feel?"

She opened her mouth to speak, but only a moan escaped, and then she tried again, managing to murmur, "Delicious."

"You are delicious."

He clutched her hips, holding her up, as his mouth devoured her. She shuddered, whimpered, threaded her fingers through his hair and gripped tight.

"I need you," he murmured against her pulsing flesh.

"Aye," she moaned.

Samuel stood before her and lifted her into the air. Instinctively, she wrapped her legs around his hips.

"Put me down, ye'll hurt yourself," she protested.

"With you I feel invincible. Nothing can hurt me."

No one had ever spoken to her the way Samuel did. He made her feel so special, cherished. It was exquisite.

He laid her on the bed and crawled up the length of her, but grimaced when he braced himself on his elbows. "Love, I don't think…"

"Oh," she said, trying to hide her disappointment. "I thought it was too soon."

"Nay, 'tis not that, I only think we need to try this in a different position." He rolled onto his back, lifting her to straddle him. "Like this."

"I didn't know…"

"And I'm glad to be the first to show you."

She smiled down at him. "I'm glad, too."

He gripped his shaft and slid it along her folds, making her eyes roll into the back of her head as she lifted her hips. He placed the head of his cock at her entrance and tilting his hips slowly slid himself inside her.

Catriona arched her spine, her head falling back as decadent pleasure gripped her. She spread her thighs wider and sank deeper against him, letting him fill her entirely.

Samuel held her, but only needed to urge her subtly to move as with the first roll of her hips a whirlwind of sensation crashed over her from her center outward. She rocked back and forth, meeting each of his thrusts.

Samuel slid his hand up her arm, over her shoulder to the back of her neck and tugged her down for a kiss. His lovemaking was slow, deliberate and with every thrust, she felt her body igniting until the blaze was so incredibly vast she could barely breathe.

"That's it, love," he murmured against her mouth. "Let it come."

What was it that was coming?

He palmed her breast, moving his lips to her nipple, and she gripped his arms, afraid to touch his chest. Sparks flew this way and that inside her, her thighs trembled uncontrollably and then she felt it, what he'd said was coming, as molten heat and pleasure crashed together in a fiery explosion between her thighs.

Her entire body convulsed, and a cry tore from her lips that was both animalistic and purely human at the same time. Saint's blood, but this was unearthly. She rode out the pleasure of his lovemaking, but the sparks did not die down, and when Samuel thrust harder, his mouth falling open on a growl and shout of his own, she found her pleasure again.

"Oh my God, love," Samuel panted.

Catriona collapsed, making sure to slide to the side of him that was not injured. She could barely move and her legs still trembled, between her thighs was still hot with liquid pleasure.

"That was amazing," she said. "Incredible."

"The best," he said. "The absolute best."

"I want to do it again," she whispered against his shoulder. "Especially that thing ye did with your tongue."

"Saints, love, but I thought you'd never ask."

Epilogue

Six months later...

CASTLE Buchanan was once more teeming with life—and absent of English knights save for one.

Catriona watched from an upstairs window as her husband dismounted from his horse in the courtyard and clapped her brother Gregor on the back. Samuel wore a Buchanan plaid and no shirt—and was the most delicious plaid-wearing man she'd ever seen. They were both covered in sweat and mud from the day's training.

After Daniel and Magnus had rid the castle of Sir Geoffrey and his violent regiment, and when Samuel was well enough to travel, they'd returned to her castle. They'd not left nor did they have plans to leave in the future. Gregor had eagerly sought Samuel's advice on fortifications and training the men, and requested that they both stay on for a while.

Samuel had agreed. An agreement that Catriona was slightly surprised at. When they'd had what everyone thought to be their second wedding ceremony at the kirk at Blair Castle, she'd expected that soon he'd be taking them back to England. Which, she admitted fully terrified her.

But when she'd asked him, Samuel had told her he had no plans to return. That eventually, when his father passed, he'd be given the title of Baron de Mowbray, a title which would pass to their eldest son, but that even when that happened, he'd hire a steward to take care of the manor.

Catriona smiled down at him. She loved this time of day best. Just before supper when Samuel came upstairs and cleaned up and they made love. Their passion had only grown and their evening adventures were never dull, but filled with pleasure.

A messenger rode from the gate toward Gregor, his face concerned as he handed over a missive. Words were exchanged that she couldn't hear and then Gregor was turning toward Samuel. They shook their heads, and spoke to the messenger once more who also shook his head.

Her belly did a little flip. Something was wrong.

She left their chamber, not willing to wait until he came to her to find out what was happening. She met him halfway on the stairs.

"What has happened?" she asked, her head pounding, stomach fluttering.

Samuel smiled. "I have been offered a post."

"A post?"

Samuel grinned from ear to ear. "Aye, love. A Highland post."

"By who?" She frowned.

"The king."

What in the world was he talking about? "Longshanks?"

"Aye."

She shook her head still confused. "And this is good?"

He nodded and let out a short laugh. "Odd actually. I wrote to him and gave him my report of Geoffrey's abhorrent behavior, and to advise him that I'd married a Scottish lass."

Her stomach plummeted. He'd confessed to the brutal king? "And he did not send for your arrest? For your execution?"

"Nay, in fact, 'tis quite backwards, but he applauds my efforts to breed with a Scot."

She gasped with outrage and smacked his shoulder. "That is not funny."

"I find it hilarious. As does Gregor."

Catriona crossed her arms over her chest. "What is the post?"

"He wants me to be a liaison between the Scots and English in the north."

"What does that mean?"

Samuel's grin widened and he lifted her into the air, planting a hot kiss on her lips. "It means I won't be arrested."

She narrowed her gaze. "Yet."

"'Haps, but I'll take it. I rather like having a head. And I rather like my Scots wife."

Catriona wasn't yet convinced the king didn't have ulterior motives. "What happened to Sir Geoffrey?"

"Well, he was recalled to England briefly, but I believe he'll be back."

Cold fear gripped her spine. She knew Samuel was capable of protecting her, and that Gregor's army was strong. Now they'd be prepared, but still... "He will be dangerous for us."

Samuel nodded.

"Where is your post?" She didn't want to leave Buchanan, but she supposed her brother would eventually want to marry and his wife would not want her sister-by-marriage stepping on her toes.

"Here for now."

"At Castle Buchanan?"

"Aye." Samuel looked sheepish and shrugged.

"What are ye not telling me?"

"'Twas Gregor's idea." Samuel sounded like a child trying to explain the reason why he'd swiped all the honey buns.

"What?"

"Your brother told me to tell the king that I'd returned and taken the castle back from the Scots and that I had Gregor well in hand."

She pushed a little on his shoulders. "So the king thinks ye've simply taken Geoffrey's place?"

"Aye."

"Why would Gregor ask ye to do such a thing?"

"Because it will protect our people," Gregor said behind Samuel. "It keeps us all safe."

"Ye're a double agent," Catriona said to her husband. The thought did not make her happy; it terrified her.

"Nay, lass. I am all for the Scots. Longshanks can kiss my arse."

Gregor laughed and moved passed them. "I'll see the both of ye at dinner."

When her brother was out of sight, Samuel took her back into his arms. "Do not be afraid, love. I will protect you. No other English bastard will ever set foot in this castle again. And with me here, I can help keep Scotland protected. The king never need know that I do not believe in his cause. Trust me, love. I'd never do anything to cause you harm. Now we know Longshanks will not come after me."

"And if he does, I will do my best to protect ye."

"I know you will." He pressed his lips to hers, and she could feel the pull of passion trying to drag her away from her thoughts.

She pushed against his shoulders again. "Samuel..."

He lifted her into the air and started to walk up the stairs. "You worry too much, lass. All will be well. We've got each other. We've got the support of the Scots." He nuzzled her neck. "We've got love and passion."

"God, I love ye," she said, letting herself fall under his charm and knowing that there would only be a glorious end. She could worry about the English king and their enemies later.

Samuel pushed open their chamber door, kicked it shut behind him and then strode straight toward the tub. He stripped her down, and then shed his own clothes, before pulling her into the warm, soapy bath and settling her on his lap.

"I plan to show you just how much I love you for the rest of the afternoon."

"And I will revel in it," Catriona said, wrapping her arms around his neck and kissing him soundly.

If you enjoyed **THE HIGHLANDER'S CHARM**, *please spread the* *word by leaving a review on the site where you purchased your copy, or a reader site such as Goodreads or Shelfari! I love to hear from readers too, so drop me a line at* authorelizaknight@gmail.com *OR visit me on Facebook:* https://www.facebook.com/elizaknightauthor. I'm also on Twitter: @ElizaKnight. If you'd like to receive my occasional newsletter, please sign up at www.elizaknight.com. *Many thanks!*

Excerpt from The Highlander's Temptation

Prologue

Spring, 1282
Highlands, Scotland

THEY GALLOPED THROUGH THE EERIE moonlit night. Warriors cloaked by darkness. Blending in with the forest, only the occasional glint of the moon off their weapons made their presence seem out of place.

'Twas chilly for spring, and yet, they rode hard enough the horses were lathered with sweat and foaming at the mouth. But the Montgomery clan wasn't going to be pushed out of yet another meeting of the clans, not when their future depended on it. This meeting would put their clan on the map, make them an asset to their king and country. As it was, years before King Alexander III had lost one son and his wife. He'd not remarried and the fate of the country now relied on one son who didn't feel the need to marry. The prince toyed with his life as though he had a death wish, fighting, drinking, and carrying on without a care in the world. The king's only other chance at a succession was his daughter who'd married but had not yet shown any signs of a bairn filling her womb. If something were to happen to the king, the country would erupt into chaos. Every precaution needed to be taken.

Young Jamie sat tall and proud upon his horse. Even prouder was he, that his da, the fearsome Montgomery laird, had allowed him to accompany the group of a half dozen seasoned warriors—the men who sat on his own clan council—to the meeting. The fact that his father had involved him in matters of state truly made his chest puff five times its size.

After being fostered out the last seven years, Jamie had just returned to his father's home. At age fourteen, he was ready to take on the duties of eldest son, for one day he would be laird. This was the perfect opportunity to show his da all he'd learned. To prove he was worthy.

Laird Montgomery held up his hand and all the riders stopped short. Puffs of steam blew out in miniature clouds from the horses' noses. Jamie's heart slammed against his chest and he looked from side to side to make sure no one could hear it. He was a man after all, and men shouldn't be scared of the dark. No matter how frightening the sounds were.

Carried on the wind were the deep tones of men shouting and the shrill of a woman's screams. Prickles rose on Jamie's arms and legs. They must have happened upon a robbery or an ambush. When he'd set out to attend his father, he'd not counted on a fight. Nay, Jamie merely thought to stand beside his father and demand a place within the Bruce's High Council.

Swallowing hard, he glanced at his father, trying to assess his thoughts, but as usual, the man sat stoic, not a hint of emotion on his face.

The laird glanced at his second in command and jutted his chin in silent communication. The second returned the nod. Jamie's father made a circling motion with his fingers, and several of the men fanned out.

Jamie observed the exchange, his throat near to bursting with questions. What was happening?

Finally, his father motioned Jamie forward. Keeping his emotions at bay, Jamie urged his mount closer. His father bent toward him, indicating for Jamie to do the same, then spoke in a hushed tone.

"We're nearly to Sutherland lands. Just on the outskirts, son. 'Tis an attack, I'm certain. We mean to help."

Jamie swallowed past the lump in his throat and nodded. The meeting was to take place at Dunrobin Castle. Why that particular castle was chosen, Jamie had not been privy to. Though he speculated 'twas because of how far north it was. Well away from Stirling where the king resided.

"Are ye up to it?" his father asked.

Tightening his grip on the reins, Jamie nodded. Fear cascaded along his spine, but he'd never show any weakness in front of his father, especially now that he'd been invited on this very important journey.

"Good. 'Twill give ye a chance to show me what ye've learned."

Again, Jamie nodded, though he disagreed. Saving people wasn't a chance to show off what he'd learned. He could never look at protecting another as an opportunity to prove his skill, only as a chance to make a difference. But he kept that to himself. His da would never understand. If making a difference proved something to his father, then so be it.

An owl screeched from somewhere in the distance as it caught onto its prey, almost in unison with the blood curdling scream of a woman.

His father made a few more hand motions and the rest of their party followed him as they crept forward at a quickened pace on their mounts, avoiding making any noise.

The road ended on a clearing, and some thirty horse-lengths away a band of outlaws circled a trio—a lady, one warrior, and a lad close to his own age.

The outlaws caught sight of their approach, shouting and pointing. His father's men couldn't seem to move quickly enough and Jamie watched in horror as the man, woman and child were hacked down. All three of them on the ground, the outlaws turned on the Montgomery warriors and rushed forward as though they'd not a care in the world.

Jamie shook. He'd never been so scared in his life. His throat had long since closed up and yet his stomach was threatening to purge everything he'd consumed that day. Even though he felt like vomiting, a sense of urgency, and power flooded his veins. Battle-rush, he'd heard it called by the seasoned warriors. And it was surging through his body, making him tingle all over.

The laird and his men raised their swords in the air, roaring out their battle cries. Jamie raised his sword to do the same, but a flash of gold behind a large lichen-covered boulder caught his attention. He eased his knees on his mount's middle.

What was that?

Another flash of gold — was that blonde hair? He'd never seen hair like that before.

Jamie turned to his father, intent to point it out, but his sire was several horse-lengths ahead and ready to engage the outlaws, leaving it up to Jamie to investigate.

After all, if there was another threat lying in wait, was it not up to someone in the group to seek them out? The rest of the warriors were intent on the outlaws which left Jamie to discover the identity of the thief.

He veered his horse to the right, galloping toward the boulder. A wee lass darted out, lifting her skirts and running full force in the opposite direction. Jamie loosened his knees on his horse and slowed. That was not what he'd expected. At all. Jamie anticipated a warrior, not a tiny little girl whose legs were no match for his mount. As he neared, despite his slowed pace, he feared he'd trample the little imp.

He leapt from his horse and chased after her on foot. The lass kept turning around, seeing him chasing her. The look of horror on her face nearly broke his heart. Och, he was no one to fear. But how would she know that? She probably thought he was after her like the outlaws had been after the man, woman and lad.

"'Tis all right!" he called. "I will nay harm ye!"

But she kept on running, and then was suddenly flying through the air, landing flat on her face.

Jamie ran toward her, dropping to his knees as he reached her side and she pushed herself up.

Her back shook with cries he was sure she tried hard to keep silent. He gathered her up onto his knees and she pressed her face to his *leine* shirt, wiping away tears, dirt and snot as she sobbed.

"Momma," she said. "Da!"

"Hush, now," Jamie crooned, unsure of what else he could say. She must have just watched her parents and brother get cut to the ground. Och, what an awful sight for any child to witness. Jamie shivered, at a loss for words.

"Blaney!" she wailed, gripping onto his shirt and yanking. "They hurt!"

Jamie dried her tears with the cuff of his sleeve. "Your family?" he asked.

She nodded, her lower lip trembling, green-blue eyes wide with fear and glistening with tears. His chest swelled with emotion for the little imp and he gripped her tighter.

"Do ye know who the men were?"

"Bad people," she mumbled.

Jamie nodded. "What's your name?"

She chewed her lip as if trying to figure out if she should tell him. "Lorna. What are ye called?"

"Jamie." He flashed her what he hoped wasn't a strained smile. "How old are ye, Lorna?"

"Four." She held up three of her fingers, then second guessed herself and held up four. "I'm four. How old are ye?"

"Fourteen."

"Ye're four, too?" she asked, her mouth dropping wide as she forgot the horror of the last few minutes of her life for a moment.

"Fourteen. 'Tis four plus ten."

"I want to be fourteen, too." She swiped at the mangled mop of blonde hair around her face, making more of a mess than anything else.

"Then we'd best get ye home. Have ye any other family?"

"A whole big one."

"Where?"

"Dunrobin," she said. "My da is laird."

"Laird Sutherland?" Jamie asked, trying to keep the surprise from his face. Did his father understand just how deep and unsettling this attack had been? A laird had been murdered. Was it an ambush? Was there more to it than just a band of outlaws? Were they men trying to stop the secret meeting from being held?

There would be no meeting, if the laird who'd called the meeting was dead.

"I'll take ye home," Jamie said, putting the girl on her feet and standing.

"Will ye carry me?" she said, her lip trembling again. She'd lost a shoe and her yellow gown was stained and torn. "I'm scared."

"Aye. I'll carry ye."

"Are ye my hero?" she asked, batting tear moistened lashes at him.

Jamie rolled his eyes and picked her up. "I'm no hero, lass."

"Hmm... Ye seem like a hero to me."

Jamie didn't answer. He tossed her on his horse and climbed up behind her. A glance behind showed that his father and his men had dispatched of most of the men, and a few others gave chase into the forest. They'd likely meet him at the castle as that had been their destination all along.

Squeezing his mount's sides, Jamie urged the horse into a gallop, intent on getting the girl to the safety of Dunrobin's walls, and then returning to his father.

Spotting Jamie with the lass, the guards threw open the gate. A nursemaid rushed over and grabbed Lorna from him, chiding her for sneaking away.

"What's happened?" A lad his own age approached. "Why did ye have my sister?"

Jamie swallowed, dismounted and held out his arm to the other young man. "I found her behind a boulder." Jamie took a deep breath, then looked the boy in the eye, hating the words he would have to say. "There was an ambush."

"My family?"

Jamie shook his head. He opened his mouth to tell the dreadful news, but the way the boy's face hardened, and eyes glistened, it didn't seem necessary. As it happened, he was given a reprieve from saying more when his father and men came barreling through the gate a moment later.

"Where's the laird?" Jamie's father bellowed.

"If what this lad said is true, then I may be right here," the boy said, straightening his shoulders.

Laird Montgomery's eyes narrowed, jaw tightened with understanding. "Aye, lad, ye are."

He leapt from his horse, his eyes lighting on Jamie "Where've ye been, lad? Ye scared the shite out of us." His father looked pale, shaken. Had he truly scared him so much?

"There was a lass," Jamie said, "at the ambush. I brought her home."

His father snorted. "Always a lass. Mark my words, lad. Think here." His father tapped Jamie's forehead hard with the tip of his finger. "The mind always knows better than the sword."

Jamie frowned and his father walked back toward the young laird. It was the second time that day that he'd not agreed with his father. For if a lass was in need of rescuing, by God, he was going to be her rescuer.

Chapter One

Dunrobin Castle, Scottish Highlands
Early Spring, 1297

"I'VE ARRANGED A MEETING BETWEEN Chief MacOwen and myself."

Lorna Sutherland lifted her eyes from her noon meal, the stew heavy as a bag of rocks in her belly as she met her older brother, Magnus', gaze.

"Why are ye telling me this?" she asked.

He raised dark brows as though he was surprised at her asking. What was he up to?

"I thought it important for ye to know."

She raised a brow and struggled to swallow the bit of pulverized carrot in her mouth. Her jaw hurt from clenching it, and she thought she might choke. There could only be one reason he felt the need to tell her this and she was certain she didn't want to know the answer. Gingerly, she set down her knife on her trencher and took a rather large gulp of watered wine, hoping it would help open her suddenly seized throat.

A moment later, she cocked her head innocently, and said, "Does not a laird and chief of his clan keep such talk to himself and his trusted council?" The haughty tone that took over could not be helped.

After nineteen summers, this conversation had been a long time coming. It was Aunt Fiona's fault. She'd arrived the week before, returning Heather, the youngest and wildest of the Sutherland siblings, and happened to see Lorna riding like the wind. Disgusted, her aunt marched straight to Magnus and demanded that he marry her off. Tame her, she'd said.

Lorna didn't see the problem with riding and why that meant she had to marry. So what if she liked to ride her horse standing on the saddle? She was good at it. Wasn't it important for a lass to excel in areas that she had skill?

Now granted, Lorna did admit that having her arms up in the air and eyes closed was borderline dangerous, but she'd done it a thousand times without mishap.

Even still, picturing her aunt's look of horror and how it had made Lorna laugh, didn't soften the blow of Magnus listening to their aunt's advice.

Magnus set down the leg of fowl he'd been eating and leaned forward on the table, his elbows pressing into the wood. Lorna found it hard to look him in the eye when he got like that. All serious and laird-like. He was her brother first, and chief second. Or at least, that's how she saw it. Judging from the anger simmering just beneath the surface of his clenched jaw and narrowed eyes, she was about to catch wind.

The room suddenly grew still, as if they were all wondering what he'd say—even the dogs.

He bared his teeth in something that was probably supposed to resemble a smile. A few of the inhabitants picked up superficial conversations again, trying as best they could to pretend they weren't paying attention. Others blatantly stared in curiosity.

"That is the case, save for when it involves deciding *your* future."

Oh, she was going to bait the bear. Lorna drew in a deep breath, crossed her arms over her chest and leaned away from the table. She could hardly look at him as she spoke. "Seems ye've already done just that."

Magnus' lips thinned into a grimace. "I see ye'll fight me on it."

"I dinna wish to marry." Emotion carried on every word. Didn't he realize what he was doing to her? The thought of marrying made her physically ill.

"Ye dinna wish to marry or ye dinna wish to marry MacOwen?"

By now the entire trestle table had quieted once more, and all eyes were riveted on the two of them. However she answered was going to determine the mood set in the room.

Och, she hated it when the lot of nosy bodies couldn't get enough of the family drama. Granted at least fifty percent of the time she was involved in said drama.

Lorna studied her brother, who, despite his grimace, waited patiently for her to answer.

The truth was, she did wish to marry—at some point. Having lost her mother when she was only four years old, she longed to have a child of her own, someone she could nurture and love. But that didn't mean she expected to marry *now*. And especially not the burly MacOwen who was easily twice her age, and had already married once or twice before. When she was a child she'd determined he had a nest of birds residing in his beard—and her thoughts hadn't changed much since.

She cocked her head trying to read Magnus' mind. Was it possible he was joking? He could not possibly believe she would ever agree to marry MacOwen.

Nay, Lorna wished to marry a man she could relate to. A man she could love, who might love her in return.

"I dinna wish to marry a man whose not seen a bath this side of a decade." Lorna spoke with a reasonable tone, not condescending, nor shrill, but just as she would have said the flowers looked lovely that morning. It was her way. Her subtlety often left people second guessing what they'd heard her say.

Magnus' lip twitched and she could tell he was trying to hold in his laughter. She dared not look down the table to see what the rest of her family and clan thought. In the past when she'd checked, gloated really, over their responses it had only made Magnus angrier.

Taming a bear meant not baiting him. And already she was doing just that. She flicked her gaze toward her plate, hoping the glance would appear meek, but in reality she was counting how many legumes were left on her trencher.

"Och, lass, I'm sure MacOwen has bathed at least once in the last year." Magnus' voice rumbled, filled with humor.

Lorna gritted her teeth. Of course Magnus would try and bait her in return. She should have seen that coming.

"And I'm sure there's another willing lass who'll scrape the filth from his back, but ye willna find her here. Not where I'm sitting."

Magnus squinted a moment as if trying to read into her mind. "But ye will agree to marry?"

Lorna crossed her arms over her chest. Lord, was her brother ever stubborn. "Not him."

"Shall we parade the eligible bachelors of the Highlands through the great hall and let ye take your pick?"

Lorna rolled her eyes, imagining just such a scene. It was horrifying, embarrassing. How many would there be in various states of dress and countenance? Some unkempt and others impeccable. Men who were pompous and arrogant or shy or annoying. Nay, thank you. She was about to spit a retort that was likely to burn her Aunt Fiona's ears when the matron broke in.

"My laird, 'haps after the meal I could speak with Lorna about marriage…in a somewhat more private arena?" Aunt Fiona was using that tone she oft used when trying to reason with one of them, that of a matron who knew better. It annoyed the peas out of Lorna and she was about to say just that, when her brother gave a slight wave of his hand, drawing her attention.

Perhaps his way of ceasing whatever words were on her tongue.

Magnus flicked his gaze from Lorna to Fiona. Why did the old bat always have to stick her nose into everything? Speaking to her in private only meant the woman would try to convince Lorna to take the marriage proposition her brother suggested. And that, she absolutely wouldn't do.

"'Tis not necessary, Aunt Fiona," Lorna said, at the exact same time Magnus stated, "Verra well."

Lorna jerked her gaze back to her brother, glaring daggers at him, but he only raised his brows in such an irritating way, a slight curve on his lips, that she was certain if she didn't excuse herself that moment she'd end up dumping her stew on his head. He had agreed on purpose —to annoy her. A horrible grinding sound came from her mouth as she gritted her teeth. Like she'd thought—brother first, chief second.

"Excuse me," she said, standing abruptly, the bench hitting hard on the back of her knees as so many people held it steady in place.

"Sit down," Magnus drawled out. "And finish your supper."

Lorna glared down at him. "I've lost my appetite."

Magnus grunted and smiled. "Och, we all know that's not true."

That only made her madder. So what if she ate just as much as the warriors? The food never seemed to go anywhere. She could eat all day long and still harbor the same lad's body she'd always had. Thick thighs, no hips, flat chest and arms to rival a squire's. If only she'd had the height of a man, then she could well and truly pummel her brother like he deserved.

She sat back down slowly and stared up at Magnus, eyes wide. Was that the reason he'd suggested MacOwen? Would no other man have her?

Nestling her hands in her lap she wrung them until her knuckles turned white.

Magnus clunked down his wooden spoon. "What is it, now?"

"Why did ye choose MacOwen?" she whispered, not wishing the rest of the table to be involved in this particular conversation. Not when she felt so vulnerable.

He shrugged, avoiding her gaze. "The man asked."

"Oh." She chewed her lip, appetite truly gone. 'Twas as she thought. No one would have her.

"Lorna..."

She flicked her gaze back up to her brother. "I but wonder if any other man would have me?"

Magnus' eyes popped and he gazed on her like she'd grown a second head and then that head grew a head. "Why would ye ask that?"

She shrugged.

By now everyone had gone back to talking and eating, knowing there'd be no more juicy gossip and Lorna was grateful for that.

"Lorna, lass, ye're beautiful, talented, spirited. Ye've taken the clan by storm. I've had to challenge more than one of my warriors for staring too long."

"More than one?" She couldn't help but glance down the table wondering which men it had been. They all slobbered like dogs over their chicken.

"None of the bastards deserve ye."

She turned back to Magnus. "And yet, ye picked the MacOwen?" She raised a skeptical brow. Ugh, of all men, he was by far the worst choice for her.

Magnus winked and picked up another scoop full of stew, shoveling into his grinning mouth.

Lorna groaned, shoulders sinking. "Ye told him nay, didna ye? Ye were baiting me."

Magnus laughed around a mouth full of stew. "Ye're too easy. I'd see ye married, but not to a man older than Uncle Artair," he said, referring to their uncle who had to be nearing seventy.

"Ugh." Lorna growled and punched her brother in the arm. "How could ye do that? Ye made every bit of my hunger go away and ye know how much I love Cook's stew."

Magnus laughed. The sound boomed off the rafters and even pulled a smile from Lorna. She loved to hear him laugh, and he didn't do it often enough. When their parents died, he'd only been fourteen, and he'd been forced to take over the whole of the clan—including raising her, and her siblings. Raising her two brothers, Ronan and Blane, and then the youngest of their brood, Heather was a feat in itself, one only Magnus could have accomplished so well. In fact, the clan had prospered. She couldn't be more proud. If anyone deserved a good match, it was Magnus.

Her heart swelled with pride. "Ye're a good man, Magnus. And an amazing brother."

He reached toward her and gave her a reassuring squeeze on her shoulder. "I'll remember that the next time ye wail at me about nonsense."

Lorna jutted her chin forward. "I do not wail—and nothing I say is nonsense."

"A true Sutherland ye are. I see your appetite has returned."

Lorna hadn't even realized she'd begun eating again. She smiled and wrapped her lips around her spoon. Resisting Cook's stew was futile. The succulent bits of venison and stewed vegetables with hints of thyme and rosemary played blissfully over her tongue.

"My laird." Aunt Fiona's voice pierced the noise of the great hall.

Magnus stiffened slightly, and glanced up. Their aunt was a gem, a tremendous help, but Lorna had heard her brother comment on more than one occasion that the woman was also a grand pain in the arse. Lorna dipped her head to keep from laughing.

"Aye?" he said, focusing his attention on their aunt.

"I'd be happy to have Lorna return home with me upon my departure. Visits with me have helped Heather so much."

Lorna's head shot up, mouth falling open as she glanced from her brother to her aunt. Good God, no! Beside her on the bench, Heather kicked Lorna in the shin and made a slight gesture with her knife as though she were slitting her wrist. Lorna pressed her lips together to keep from laughing.

"I'm sure that's not necessary, Aunt," Lorna said, giving the woman her sweetest smile. At least she'd not told her there was no way in hell she'd step foot outside of this castle for a journey unless it was on some adventure she chose for herself. She'd heard enough horror stories about the etiquette lessons Heather had to endure.

"Magnus?" Fiona urged.

There was a flash of irritation in his eyes. Magnus didn't mind his siblings calling him by his name, but all others were to address him formally. Lorna agreed that should be the case with the clan, but with family, Lorna thought he ought to be more lenient, especially where their aunt was concerned.

Aye, she was a thorn in his arse, but she was also very helpful.

Before her brother could say something he'd regret, Lorna pressed her hand to his forearm and chimed in. "'Haps we can plan on me accompanying Heather on her next visit."

That seemed to pacify their aunt. She nodded and returned to her dinner.

Ronan, who sat beside Magnus on the opposite side of the table, leaned close to their brother and smirked as he said something. Probably crude. Lorna rolled her eyes. If Blane was here, he'd have joined in their bawdy drivel. Or maybe even saved her from having to invite herself to stay at their aunt's house.

As it was, Blane was gallivanting about the countryside and the borders dressed as an Englishman selling wool. Sutherland wool. Their prized product. Superior to all others in texture, softness, thickness, and ability to hold dye.

She stirred her stew, frowning. Blane always came home safe and sound, but she still worried. There was a lot of unrest throughout the country, and the blasted English king, Longshanks, was determined to be rid of them all. It would only take one wrong move and her beloved brother would be forever taken away.

Lorna glanced up. She gazed from one sibling to the next. She loved them. All of them. They loved each other more than most, maybe because they'd lost their parents so young and only had each other to rely on. Whatever the case was, they'd a bond not even steel could cut through.

Magnus raised his mug of ale. "A toast!" he boomed.

Every mug lifted into the air, ale sloshing over the sides and cheers filled the room.

"Clan Sutherland!" he bellowed.

And the room erupted in uproarious calls and clinks of mugs. A smile split her face and she was overcome with joy.

She'd be perfectly happy never to leave here. And perfectly ecstatic to never marry MacOwen.

Even still, as she clinked her mug and took a mighty gulp, she couldn't help but wonder if there was a man out there she could love, and one who just might love her in return.

*Want to read more? Check out **The Highlander's Temptation** and the rest of the **Stolen Bride** series wherever ebooks are sold...*

About the Author

Eliza (E.) Knight is an award-winning and *USA Today* bestselling author of over fifty sizzling historical romance and rip-your-heart-out historical fiction. While not reading, writing or researching for her latest book, she chases after her three children. In her spare time (if there is such a thing...) she likes daydreaming, wine-tasting, traveling, hiking, staring at the stars, watching movies, shopping and visiting with family and friends. She lives atop a small mountain with her own knight in shining armor, three princesses and two very naughty puppies. Visit Eliza at http://www.elizaknight.com or her historical blog History Undressed: www.historyundressed.com. Sign up for her newsletter to get news about books, events, contests and sneak peaks! http://eepurl.com/CSFFD

facebook.com/elizaknightfiction

twitter.com/elizaknight

instagram.com/elizaknightfiction

bookbub.com/authors/eliza-knight

goodreads.com/elizaknight